cupcake cousins

Summer Showers

Also by Kate Hannigan

Cupcake Cousins

cupcake cousins

Summer Showers

by Kate Hannigan

illustrated by
Brooke Boynton Hughes

DISNEP • HYPERION
LOS ANGELES | NEW YORK

First Edition, June 2015

10 9 8 7 6 5 4 3 2 1

G475-5664-5-15074

Printed in the United States of America

Library of Congress Cataloging-in-Publication Data

Hannigan, Kate.

Summer showers / by Kate Hannigan ; illustrated by Brooke Boynton Hughes.

pages cm.—(Cupcake cousins ; 2)

Summary: "Cousins Willow and Delia return to the kitchen as their family welcomes a new baby in the second book in the illustrated Cupcake Cousins series"—Provided by publisher.

ISBN 978-1-4847-1662-5 (hardback)—ISBN 1-4847-1662-0

[1. Baking—Fiction. 2. Cousins—Fiction. 3. Family life—Michigan—Fiction. 4. Michigan, Lake—Fiction.] I. Hughes, Brooke Boynton, illustrator. II. Title.

PZ7.H198158Su 2015

[Fic]—dc23   2014044882

Reinforced binding

Visit www.DisneyBooks.com

Publisher's Note: The recipes contained in this book are to be followed exactly as written, under adult supervision. The Publisher is not responsible for your specific health or allergy needs that may require medical supervision. The Publisher is not responsible for any adverse reactions to the recipes contained in this book.

SUSTAINABLE FORESTRY INITIATIVE   Certified Sourcing   www.sfiprogram.org   SFI-00993

THIS LABEL APPLIES TO TEXT STOCK

for gabriel and nolan,
philip and jeffrey—sweet williams, all
—k.h.

for laura, julie, and katie
—b.b.h.

Contents

· The Bumpus Family ·
invites you to join in celebrating
a baby shower
for

Rose & Jonathan Bumpus-Baxter

at 12 o'clock noon
on Saturday, June 29th

in the shared yards of
Whispering Pines Bed & Breakfast
and the newly opened
Arts & Eats Café
in Saugatuck, Michigan

Chapter 1
let the summering begin!

delia stopped pacing across the wide white porch and froze where she was standing. Her ears had finally caught the very particular noise she'd been waiting hours to hear. It was the sound of gravel crunching beneath car wheels. And it meant not one, not two, but three very important things.

"Willow's here!" she shouted, racing down the steps and into the yard. "They're all here! We can start summer vacation now!"

Delia's parents, Delvan and Deenie Dees, appeared in the yard, waving as three cars pulled over to the parking area beneath the tall pine trees.

One car was holding Willow, along with the rest of the Sweeney family. Another car belonged to Grandma and Grandpa Bumpus, who Delia loved like crazy too. And the third carried Aunt Rosie and Jonathan—*Uncle* Jonathan, Delia had to remind herself—who were going to have a baby soon. Rosie and Jonathan were the big reason the family was getting together so early in the summer. And *big* barely described it.

Delia took one look at her aunt's beach-ball belly and could hardly find the right words. It was enormous.

Tremendous. HUMONGOUS! It was so big in fact that the doctor said Aunt Rosie was going to have her baby early, which was why the shower was moved up to Saturday—just three days away.

Aunt Rosie heaved a heavy sigh as she tried to pull herself out of the car. Finally, she gave up and reached out her arms for help. Delia's dad took hold and gently tugged her from the front seat.

"I can't wait to meet our new cousin," Delia said, stepping over and giving Aunt Rosie a hug. Or it was more like she *tried* to give her a hug, but Aunt Rosie's belly got in the way. "We'll show her everything about Whispering Pines. The hummingbirds and fireflies, blueberry bushes and the dunes on the beach!"

"What makes you think this baby is a girl?" asked Aunt Rosie with a grin.

"Could be a boy," added Uncle Jonathan, who had come around the car and was beside her now. "We're not telling anybody anything!"

Delia begged to be in on their secret. But Aunt Rosie and Uncle Jonathan just made zipping motions over their lips. They wanted to surprise the whole family once the baby was born.

"The Chicago caravan made it," called Delia's mom as family spilled out onto the lawn. "I'm so glad you all came together."

"We wanted to be there in case Rosie had her baby on the way," said Willow's mom, Aunt Aggie Sweeney. And she threw her arms around Delia's mother. Delia greeted her next, careful not to get poked by one of the pencils that were always tucked in Aunt Aggie's hair.

"*Deeee*-lia!" came a shout. "Where are you?"

While Delia loved thinking about the newest cousin who would join the Bumpus family, she couldn't forget her favorite one. She raced past Grandma and Grandpa in their floppy sun hats, planting quick pecks on their cheeks as she darted by. She zigzagged around Willow's big sister, Violet, who had moments of being fun but was mostly crabby. Delia figured that's what made her a perfect match for her own big sister, Darlene, who was chewing bubble gum beside her.

Then she weaved her way past her little cousin, Sweet William, and the Sweeney family dog, Bernice, an enormous Bernese mountain dog that Delia considered a cousin, too. Only hairy and with a drooling problem, but just as wonderful.

"We're happy to be out of the car," Sweet William announced, hopping up and down like a frog with Bernice. Delia did a quick frog hop herself, since she was happy they were out of the car too. In fact, everybody seemed excited to be in Saugatuck, stretching their legs beneath the tall trees and breathing in the fresh lake air.

When Delia finally spotted copper curls and a polka-dotted bag, she wanted to laugh and sing and whoop all at the same time.

"Willow! I'm right here!" she called, waving.

And Delia started to launch into a flying hug. But catching sight of a white bandage on Willow's hand, she stopped short. "What happened?"

Willow shrugged and tried to push the hair out of her eyes. But her bandage—layers of gauze wrapped around a thin splint that held the pinkie, ring, and tall-guy fingers on Willow's right hand—made that difficult. So Delia reached over and helped.

"I did it in karate class," Willow explained, holding up her injured hand and studying it. "You might not guess from the way my fingers look, but I broke the board."

Willow was beaming, and that made Delia smile just as broadly. There was always something about Willow that made Delia feel fizzy inside, like she was on the verge of laughing. And suddenly they tumbled onto the lawn as they always did, chittering and rolling and carrying on like a couple of happy squirrels. How else was summer vacation supposed to start?

"Some things never change," came a voice from above them. And Delia didn't even have to look up to know that Darlene and Violet were standing there. "You two might have saved Aunt Rosie's wedding cake last summer, but you're still just a couple of silly flower girls."

"Make that *flour* girls," said Willow. "You know,

the cooking kind." And that made Delia laugh all over again.

With their sunglasses low on their noses, the big sisters rolled their eyes to the leafy green treetops. Darlene let out a *pfff* like a teakettle, and Violet adjusted the strap of a bulky bag over her shoulder—Delia thought it was shaped like a miniature guitar. And together they trudged off toward the rest of the family like they had important business to attend to.

"I can't wait to hear you play your ukulele," Delia overheard her sister telling Violet. "Maybe we can perform for customers at the café. With you on the strings and me singing, we could be a great duo. We'll have to come up with a catchy name!"

Now it was Willow and Delia's turn for eye rolling.

They helped each other to their feet, standing in the center of the yards that connected Whispering Pines Bed & Breakfast with Delia's new home next door. Last year they'd called that droopy house the old Sutherland place, but now it was the Arts & Eats Café, a name she and Willow had helped pick.

Willow dropped her bag in the grass, and the two cousins kicked off their sandals and slipped onto the lowest branches of a nearby tree. They were high enough to take in the view of Lake Michigan spreading out in endless blue beyond the green lawn.

"Can you get any higher with your hand like that?" asked Delia, making room on a wide bough just above Willow.

Holding on with her left hand, Willow swung her legs onto Delia's branch and hung upside down. Her long curls sprang from her head like Slinky toys.

"It's fine," Willow said, adjusting the gauze around her injured fingers. "It hurt Monday when I did it. But it's been a couple days already, so it's no big deal."

Birds high overhead began chirping and chatting, almost as much as the cousins perched below. Delia told Willow about her new school, as well as her new house, new friends, new everything since they'd left Detroit.

"See the sign over there in the front yard?" she asked, hooking her legs and dangling upside down

beside Willow. She pointed off toward the yellow house, where the funky ARTS & EATS CAFÉ sign swung in the breeze. "It's made of glass and rocks and paint-brushes. My mom and I put it together."

Delia watched her mom and Aunt Aggie slowly climb the café steps, Aunt Rosie and her beach-ball belly between them.

"I can't believe how big Aunt Rosie is," Willow

said, pulling herself upright on the branch. "It's a little creepy, don't you think? The whole baby thing?"

"What do you mean, Willow? We're going to have a new cousin any day now!"

Willow said she was excited about a cousin, just not the baby part. "It's like she swallowed a watermelon—whole!"

Willow shuddered, which made Delia laugh. She told Willow how much fun the baby shower was going to be with everyone in town to celebrate. It was just a few days away, and there would be lots of presents and people and good food.

"I've been thinking about Aunt Rosie's party too," Willow said, dropping out of the tree onto the cushiony grass. "I hope we can find a way to do something special for it."

Delia slid down from the branch. With Willow's hand injured, would she still be able to use a spatula? Operate a mixer? Hold on to a measuring cup? Delia didn't want to hurt Willow's feelings, but she had to ask: "Can you even cook?"

"The only thing that's tricky is cracking eggs," Willow said. "But my dad taught me how to do that with my left hand. So we can still bake as much as we want this summer."

Delia was relieved to hear it. Because of all the things she loved about her new life here along the water, her absolute-very-best-most-favorite-number-one thing was still the same: being in the Whispering Pines kitchen with Willow.

"I like the idea of helping with Aunt Rosie's shower," Delia said as patches of sunlight played hopscotch on the grass. "And I want to help out with the new café too—I have a little plan for that."

She paused, thinking about telling Willow more. But there would be time later—maybe after dinner, when the sun was setting. Now was the time to talk about all the fun they would have together, not for what might happen if Delia had to move again.

"Let's make sure this summer is different from last year's," she said with a smile. "And that means no confusing the ingredients, no hungry dogs alone with bacon, and no exploding blenders!"

"It's a deal," Willow said, her whole body bouncing in excitement.

And they shook on it. Though with Willow's injured fingers, they had to use their left hands.

Delia looked into her cousin's happy face and felt that same fizzy urge to laugh again. Putting her worries aside, she grinned right back at Willow. "This summer, there's nothing we can't do!"

Chapter 2
a mess already?

There's nothing she can do with that hand," Willow's mom was saying, "except let it heal. It's such a shame it happened right at the start of summer, too."

The cousins were wandering around Delia's new backyard now. Delia had just bent down to scratch Bernice's ears when she overheard the grown-ups talking. Willow was a few steps behind her, looking at a worm Sweet William found. What did Aunt Aggie mean about Willow's hand? Was she supposed to stay out of the kitchen this week? How was that even possible?

"I agree," said Delia's mom, who was a nurse at the nearby hospital. "I took a look at her fingers, and I don't think the girls will be able to do much in the kitchen this summer until that bandage and splint come off. It's too bad."

The three sisters were seated on the café's back porch, propping up Aunt Rosie's swollen feet. But as Willow got closer, Delia decided to point her away from the porch and toward the bluff, where she wouldn't overhear the grown-ups' conversation.

The cousins had already explored the grounds over at Whispering Pines—starting with Mr. Henry's hobby shed and Cat's vegetable garden. Henry Rickles was the owner of Whispering Pines Bed & Breakfast. But since the whole Bumpus family had been coming here every summer since Delia's mom, Aunt Aggie, and Aunt Rosie were babies, Mr. Henry was more like family. And now that he and Catherine Sutherland, the Whispering Pines caterer, were going to get married, suddenly Cat was family, too.

"Where did the fence go?" asked Willow as they

walked along where the two yards met.

"Mr. Henry took it down," Delia explained. "He didn't want anything coming between him and Cat."

"So she's living with you guys in the yellow house?" wondered Willow.

"She's on the top floor," Delia explained, stopping to examine a bluish-black butterfly that had landed nearby. "But it's just until their wedding—at Christmas or New Year's or something. Then she'll move over to Whispering Pines."

They crossed toward the blueberry bushes on the far side of Delia's property, peeking deep into shrubs along the way in search of hummingbird nests. Standing along the bluff's edge, they looked down at the waves below and tried not to get dizzy. Delia picked cherries off a fruit tree Grandma had rescued near the house.

"Here, catch," she said, tossing a cherry in Willow's direction.

"Thanks," Willow said, catching it expertly with her good hand.

Delia couldn't help but smile. Willow's right hand might need a rest, but she could still do plenty of things with her left one.

Delia didn't doubt her cousin for even a moment. Why should she?

"Come on, I can't wait to show you the new kitchen," she said, looping arms with Willow and setting off for the pretty yellow porch. With her cousin finally here for the next week, it really felt like summer vacation. "Maybe we can make some chocolate brownies? Or carrot cake with veggies from Cat's garden?"

Delia was proud of the way the old Sutherland house was coming along. It used to look run-down and a little spooky when Cat was trying to take care of things on her own. Now, with her parents and Cat working together to replace the old wood and put on a fresh coat of paint, it was like a whole new place. They had turned the downstairs into an art gallery for Delia's dad and a café for Cat. And since her family had moved in upstairs, well, the yellow house seemed just about perfect to Delia.

"You don't have to worry about these stairs any-more," she said brightly. And she felt a little bounce in her step like Willow as she climbed the wooden porch stairs. Just last summer, they were broken and dangerous.

Waving as they passed the three aunts, Delia turned the knob and led Willow into the big living room. It served as the main gallery of the Arts & Eats Café, and her dad's artwork was hanging everywhere. When Willow had come for a quick visit months ago, the house was still being repaired. But finally, thankfully, the remodeling was complete.

"*Ta-da!*" Delia said with a smile.

"This place is amazing. It's like a dream come true for Uncle Delvan," Willow said, walking from one colorful canvas to the next. "I bet his paintings are flying out the door."

Delia's dad was across the room, smiling at the two cousins. He was leading his own tour of the house for Uncle Liam and Uncle Jonathan.

"Running a business is hard work, Willow," he explained. "We're always trying to get more people to stop in and taste Cat's amazing food. And maybe they'll take a liking to my art, too. So it is a dream come true that I get to paint every day, you're right about that," he said, giving his goatee a thoughtful scratching. "But my art isn't exactly flying out the door."

Just then, something really did go flying out the door, bolting across the gallery's wooden floors and down the back porch steps. It was brown and black and white and furry.

And it was followed by a curly haired boy.

"Sweet William!" Willow hollered after them. "What are you doing? You and Bernice left squishy footprints all over the floor!"

The uncles went chasing after Sweet William and Bernice, while Delia and Willow followed the messy marks back up the hallway. They led into a kitchen.

A modern, silvery kitchen.

Cat's new kitchen.

"What do you two whippersnappers think you're doing?"

Delia stopped short, causing Willow to smack right into the back of her. Together they stood at the edge of the room, frozen with fear. Was Cat angry with them already? What had they done?

"W-we were just trying to cook . . ." came a voice.

". . . something to serve for breakfast," came another.

It was their big sisters!

"Are they crazy?" whispered Willow. "Violet doesn't know her way around a kitchen. She can't even boil water without burning it!"

Delia told her to "*shhhhh.*" Cat was starting to talk again.

"I don't know what you two were hoping to make," Cat was telling Darlene and Violet. "But from the looks of it, y'all made a mess." And with Cat's Southern way of talking, it came out sounding like *may-esss.*

Delia and Willow inched their heads around the corner for a glimpse. And what they saw made their jaws drop. Because it wasn't just a regular, ordinary mess. It was a spectacular one.

A big pot was sitting on the stove, and something had overflowed. Delia squinted to see what it was.

"Oatmeal?" she whispered.

It had oozed over the rim and was dripping down the sides of the pot like lava spilling from a volcano. It glooped into a lumpy pile on the stove top, trailing down the front of the oven. And globs of it had fallen onto the floor, which is probably how Sweet William had stepped in it with his bare feet. Bernice, too.

"That's disgusting," Willow whispered, pulling back around the corner and leaning against the wall. "Were our disasters last summer as bad as that one?"

Delia tried not to think too much about their cooking disasters.

"Y'all better grab some towels and a mop," Cat ordered their sisters. "Because you're gonna be

busier than gophers on a golf course."

Delia pointed toward the staircase and they tip-toed off. "Let's leave those two to Cat," she whispered. "I'll show you more of the house. It's been a few months since you've seen everything."

Chapter 3
delia's sunny yellow house

They dashed upstairs and peeked into the bedrooms on the second and third floors. Delia showed Willow her room with its bright green walls hung with animal posters, along with photos pinned to a cork bulletin board. There were pictures of her and Willow from last summer, her and Willow from Christmas, her and Willow from Grandpa's birthday party. She was especially proud of the bookshelves that took up one entire wall. Her dad had built them to help organize all her books, which she liked to trade with Aunt Aggie, since Willow's mom was a school librarian and knew

Not-So-Gloopy Breakfast Parfaits

Ingredients:
2 cups oatmeal (not the instant kind)
4 cups milk
2 cups fruit (whatever you have on hand)
2 cups yogurt (any flavor you like)

Directions:
1. Make sure you have an adult's help.

2. Put the oatmeal and milk in a pot, and bring to a boil. Lower the heat to just above a simmer, and cook for about 7 minutes, stirring as needed. Make sure you don't leave it on high, or your oatmeal will overflow the pot and make a gloopy mess that your dog or your brother is sure to step in.

3. When the oatmeal has cooked, pour it into a bowl and set it in the refrigerator to cool.

4. Select your fruit. (Willow likes blueberries; Delia's favorites are strawberries.) Slice the fruit, if necessary, to the size of a coin. Set aside.

5. Once the oatmeal has cooled, choose a serving glass. Mason jars make for a pretty presentation, but any glass will do. Begin by spooning ¼ cup yogurt on the bottom of your glass. Next spoon ¼ cup oatmeal on top of it. Then layer in the fruit.

6. Repeat until you reach the top of your glass. Then grab a spoon and enjoy!

Makes 4 parfaits.

everything about good books.

"Are you going to zoo camp again this summer?" Willow asked, running her fingers (the good ones) across the shelves.

Delia plopped onto her beanbag chair and shook her head. There weren't any zoos near Saugatuck, she told Willow, not like when they lived in Detroit and could go to the big zoo there. But she didn't mind. Who needed zoo camp when Gossie, their adopted Canada goose, was around?

"Having Gossie is like having zoo camp in your own backyard," she explained.

"That's another great thing about living here," Willow said, peering out the window overlooking the two yards.

Delia agreed. And she couldn't help but rattle off a long list of the things she liked best since they moved here: the way the waves froze in midsplash during the coldest part of winter, how a rain owl had adopted the trees just outside her window. "And the after-school zoology club and helping Mr. Henry's brother,

Reverend Rickles, bag groceries for the soup kitchen. Oh, and getting picked to be a crossing guard again."

Then, barely missing a beat, she added, "And, of course, I saved the best for last: having you come visit!"

Willow grinned and flopped onto Delia's bed. "Can we sleep in your room sometime this week? I want to pretend like I live here all the time, the way you do."

Delia said they could sleep here or over at Whispering Pines or even in a tent in the backyard. "Wherever you'd like, Willow, because I want to pretend like you live here all the time, too!"

And then, the worry creeping back into her thoughts, she added more softly, "I love it here. I don't ever want to move again."

Before long, they made their way back downstairs and into the café. The walls were painted a warm, buttery color. And tables of all different sizes and shapes filled the room. Delia pointed out her dad's paintings hanging on the walls. They looked beautiful in the afternoon sunshine.

"But there's only one customer," Willow whispered. "Is that how it usually is around here?"

Delia nodded, tugging on her braided ponytail. She felt a knot begin to form in her stomach.

"I've never once seen it crowded here," she said softly. "Cat and my dad, they're trying. But it's not easy. They've got to do something to let people know about Arts and Eats. *We've* got to, Willow."

Both girls looked around the empty restaurant. Everything was neat and in order, ready for customers.

Delia inhaled the familiar aroma of brewed coffee. And the food in the display case looked delicious— Cat had made tomato sandwiches, apple salads, spinach quiche, and mushroom turnovers.

But nobody was there to eat them.

"At this rate, the café could be out of business by the end of summer," Delia said, her eyes suddenly wet. She quickly blinked the tears away. "I don't know what my dad will do without the art gallery. He's so happy now, and my mom too. They're even going on morning jogs together—the way they used to. Willow, I don't know what I'll do if we have to leave this place and move away."

Willow turned to face Delia, only she wasn't bouncing on her toes like she so often did. Delia could see the determination in Willow's eyes. They were the same eyes she had: amber with thick black lashes, just like Grandpa's. That's how she and Willow saw things the same way.

That's how they were closer than cousins, stronger than sisters, even bigger than best friends.

"I see what you're talking about, Delia," she whispered. "And I promise, I'll help you do anything I can for the café. Because I love it here too!"

"I was hoping you'd say that," Delia said quietly, looking around to make sure no one overheard, "because I have a plan."

Delia had just started to explain it as they stepped out onto the back porch. But she didn't get far, as Grandma's "yoo-hoo" called them over. Violet and Darlene were already tucked into a porch swing nearby, lolling lazily back and forth. Sweet William and Bernice were seated near Grandma's feet.

"Girls, go sit down with your grandmother," Delia's mom was saying from the other end of the porch with her sisters. "She has something special to share with you."

"And be careful you don't bump your hand!" called Aunt Aggie. "I don't want you hurting it all over again."

Delia slipped into a chair and made room for

Willow to scoot in beside her. She would have to wait until later to tell Willow about the plan to help the café. Now she was wondering what Grandma's *something special* was: tulip bulbs? A rare flowering vine? Maybe an apple tree?

"With Rosie and Jonathan's baby almost here, I wanted to take a moment for you," Grandma began. "This baby is going to get a lot of attention soon. But I want to make sure the rest of you grandchildren know how special you are to me."

And removing her green gardening gloves, Grandma slipped her hand into her vest pocket. When she pulled it out, there were pieces of jewelry resting in her palm. She laid them delicately in her lap.

"I was doing a bit of tidying up before we left Chicago, and I decided I'd pass along a few Bumpus family heirlooms to you five grandkids. Some of these are a hundred years old," she said.

She started with Sweet William, handing him a small pocket watch and explaining how it once belonged to her father. "He was brave and clever, just like you," she said. Then she picked up a pretty silver charm bracelet and put it on Darlene's slim wrist. She told her that it came from her favorite aunt, Josephine, who was a dancer too.

"As we welcome the newest member, I think it's good for us to think about what family means," Grandma explained. "That's because every member of a family helps shape us, in one way or another."

For Violet, she had a pair of pearl earrings that had been made by Grandpa's uncle Lou. "He was a deep-sea diver," Grandma said. "Got these pearls from the bottom of the ocean. I think they'll look good on you, but don't go swimming in them."

Violet and Darlene thanked Grandma, and Sweet William stood up and gave her a bear hug. Now there were just two more pieces left on her lap. Delia wondered which was for her and which was for Willow.

"I want you to have this necklace, Willow," Grandma said. "It was mine." And Willow kneeled beside Grandma's chair as she hooked the clasp, letting the tiny golden pendant of a daisy dangle around

Willow's neck. "You're cheerful like a daisy and full of energy, just like I was."

"You still are, Grandma," Willow reminded.

Finally it was Delia's turn.

"And lastly, for you," Grandma continued, slipping something delicate and gold onto Delia's finger,

"I want you to have this ring. It belonged to my mother, who was smart and steady, just like you."

Now it was Delia and Willow's turn for bear hugs and thank-yous. All five cousins marveled at their new gifts, showing them to their moms and aunts and each other. They promised Grandma they would take good care of their heirlooms.

"We'll go right up to Darlene's room and put these away," announced Violet, putting her hand on Sweet William's shoulder and steering him toward the door. "We don't want anything getting lost, especially since Darlene and I are going to be busy working in the café this week."

Delia let out a gasp and Willow gulped, so together they sounded like a startled toad.

"What do you mean you're going to be working at the café?" Delia asked, her voice tight.

Darlene was looking at the different charms dangling from her bracelet. "Of course we are," she said. "I'm a teenager now, and Violet practically is. This could be like a summer job. We're not going to spend the week goofing off like you two."

Violet leaned on Darlene's shoulder and tried to stand as tall as her older cousin.

"We can run the cash register, serve the food, even do some of the cooking," she began. Then, turning her gaze fully on Willow and her injured hand, she added, "You can't do anything now anyway. So Darlene and I will make things—you know, parfaits, cookies, desserts."

They turned and stepped into the house, followed by their mothers, who were gently easing enormous Aunt Rosie into the air-conditioned café for a lemonade. Grandma pulled her green gardening gloves back on as she waved good-bye and headed off to her azalea bushes in the yard.

"Parfaits?" said Willow.

"Cookies?" wondered Delia.

"Desserts!" they both exclaimed.

Willow and Delia stared into each other's faces, stunned by what their sisters had just announced.

"Desserts are what *we* do!" Willow yelped. "They

can have anything else, but not desserts!"

Delia put her hands on Willow's shoulders and told her not to worry. But inside, the knot in her stomach was pulling tighter than ever. *Family helps shape us*, Grandma had said. Delia couldn't help but feel like their big sisters were going to do just that to her and Willow—only with a rolling pin.

Chapter 4
batter splatter

It was later that day when Delia and Willow climbed
the staircase up the bluff from the beach, where they
had spent a good, long while walking and talking and
looking for sea glass.

"The County Fair is this week," Delia said, a little
breathless from the steep stairs. "It's the biggest deal
of the summer."

"After Aunt Rosie's baby shower, of course," reminded Willow.

"Of course!" Delia agreed as they reached the top
step. "But they have these contests I want to tell you
about. This is the plan I've been working out in my

head: I was thinking that if we could come up with something really special to bake, maybe you and I could enter."

"A contest?" Willow said with a grin. "I like the sound of that."

But before Delia could go on, Mr. Henry and Cat were waving them over. Grandma stood beside them, her hat ringed with bright marigolds.

"Howdy, y'all!" called Cat across the yard. And it looked to Delia like she was handing out cigars. "Come on over here—we need your taste buds!"

The cousins hurried over, picking their way through the grass in bare feet.

"Good afternoon, ladies," Mr. Henry announced with a tip of his straw sun hat. "I'm delighted to see the two of you together again. We could use your opinions on a particularly promising project we've been working on."

Mr. Henry was carrying a jar in his arms. And Delia quickly realized he and Cat weren't giving out cigars, they were passing around pickles. He unscrewed the lid and held out the glass jar. "Your grandmother has been kind enough to share her thoughts. Now we'd like yours: Are they tart enough? Perhaps they need a bit more vinegar?"

"*Mmmm-mmm*," said Willow, sampling one with a noisy crunch. "Delicious. These are the best pickles I've ever tasted, Mr. Henry. And that's the truth."

Delia took one next. Crunch again.

"Willow's right," Delia said, her lips puckering. "Those are perfect pickles!"

Cat gave Mr. Henry's back an enthusiastic slap. "We've been working so hard on this project, I think my brain is pickled! It's put me behind on everything else. I haven't had a moment to make desserts for the café. And with Rosie's baby shower coming Saturday, I had to hire someone to make her cake."

"Hire someone?" choked Willow, her mouth full of pickle. "Why?"

"After seeing your hand there . . ." Cat said, her eyes on Willow's bandaged fingers. "Well, maybe I should have considered your sisters—they seem so eager to do the cooking this year."

Willow began to sputter. But before she could get out another word, Cat and Mr. Henry were talking on.

"We plan to enter these pickles in the Saugatuck County Fair this Saturday," he said, his cheeks growing a shade pinker. "I don't mean to be boastful. But with Ms. Catherine on my team, so to speak . . . well, I believe our pickles just might win a blue ribbon in the contest."

Contest? Delia's jaw dropped open. And Willow looked over with wide eyes. They were too stunned to speak.

"A blue-ribbon prize is just the sort of thing we need here at the café," he said, with a nod in Cat's direction. "If only Arts and Eats had something big to brag about, something to make diners sit up and take notice. Maybe, and dare I say it, give diners a reason to shout."

And just then, a real shout rang out. It was coming from the kitchen.

"Eeeeek! Aaaaaak! Waaaaak!"

Delia and Willow dashed up the back porch steps, racing through the gallery and around the corner. Cat and Mr. Henry were at their heels. Delia could hear bangs and thumps and "hmmphs" coming from Cat's sleek silver kitchen, like a marching band was rehearsing in there.

Only when Delia and Willow peeked around the corner, there was no band and no rehearsing.

Just big sisters. And they were at it again.

"I don't get it!" Darlene yelled, chocolatey batter dripping from her arms. Her entire shirt was spattered in brown gunk. "How is this thing supposed to work?"

Violet was covered in the same goo. She stood next to Darlene, staring at the stand mixer with a puzzled expression. "I think we're supposed to turn it on and then duck."

The wall nearest them as well as a few other appliances and a tan wooden cabinet overhead were all covered

in the same chocolate batter.

Delia and Willow slipped back around the corner and out of sight, leaving Cat and Mr. Henry to deal with their sisters.

"They were trying to cook again," whispered Willow angrily. "It looks like brownies this time. Or maybe a chocolate cake!"

"Do you realize what this means?" Delia asked in a hushed voice, her eyes as round as two doughnut holes. "First the oatmeal volcano, and now this chocolate batter flying everywhere?"

"Yes," stormed Willow, her voice a muffled shout. "Our sisters are moving in on our *thing*! They're trying to cook, just like us!"

"No," squealed Delia, hoping to keep her joy from anyone else's ears. "It means *we're* not the disasters in the kitchen this summer. *They* are!"

Chapter 5
a backyard campout

the skies were cloudy for most of the day, and a few showers rained down here and there in quick bursts. But by the time the sun went down, the lawn was dry and calling to Delia and Willow. At least, that's what they told their moms as they begged and pleaded (but never whined) to sleep outside in the yard.

"Okay," Aunt Aggie said, "but remember, the back door is unlocked in case you get scared and want to come back inside. And Willow," she added, calling after them, "give that hand of yours a rest!"

They had the tent pitched and were hammering

the last stake into the ground as the tangerine-orange sun dipped into the water. So they unrolled their sleeping bags on the grass, stretching out between Grandma's azalea bushes to the left and one of her unfinished gardening projects to the right.

The cousins might not have been in the wilderness, but the idea of sleeping outside all night felt a little wild.

"I like listening to the trees," Willow said, rolling onto her back and looking up at the top branches. Delia flopped down beside her. The wind off the lake had the leaves swaying and rustling. "I never do this sort of thing in Chicago. Too many tall buildings, too much light."

"I bet we'll hear that rain owl soon," Delia said, and she scanned the top branches in the dimming light. "It has this amazing call. You won't believe it 'til you hear it!"

The cousins tugged on their sweatshirts and pulled out a deck of cards along with a flashlight. The first stars of the night began to twinkle overhead, mixing in with the fireflies glimmering around them. As they dealt hand after hand of crazy eights, Delia took comfort in the sounds of the waves lapping on the shore below and the occasional laughter of their moms.

"Your mom does seem happy," Willow began. "Not like last summer, when you were so worried about her and your dad."

Delia said her mom loved her job at the new hospital. "She says everything there is fancy and bright. Her hospital is so new, they don't even have pictures hanging up. It's just blank walls everywhere."

Willow said everything about Saugatuck seemed fancy and bright, even on cloudy days. "If only our family could live here all year, like you. But my mom and dad would never leave Chicago. So instead, I'll just come visit and stay as long as I can. You'll be my summer camp!"

Delia said she liked the sound of Camp Cousins.

"But Darlene is the one who really needs Camp Cousins," she added, slipping the ring Grandma had given her from one finger to the next. It was a little loose, even on her biggest finger. "She's been crying a lot. Nobody tells me anything, but I know she had a hard time this year, changing to the new middle school. I hope this summer, with you guys here, she'll start to feel better about things."

"Talking about sisters," Willow said, rolling onto her stomach and facing Delia. "What are we going to do about them? If they keep messing up the kitchen, we'll never get a chance to make any-thing."

Delia had been thinking about their sisters too. And she'd decided things might not be all that bad. "If they keep Cat busy over at the Arts and Eats Café, that means the Whispering Pines kitchen is—"

The snap of a twig in the dark yard made them turn their heads.

"I think someone's coming," Willow whispered. "Where's your flashlight?"

"Right here." Delia flicked the switch, sending a long yellow beam across the blue-black lawn. It landed on Delia's mom, Aunt Aggie, and Grandma, who were squinting in the glare.

"Shine that on the path, would you?" asked Aunt Aggie. "I'm afraid I'll trip on a skunk out here!"

"Don't worry about skunks," Grandma said. "Worry about my flower beds. I don't want us trampling the petunias!"

Once they reached the tent, a little breathless and full of grown-up giggling, their moms joined them on the sleeping bags. Willow and Delia made room in the middle for Grandma, giving her a double layer of extra blankets to sit on.

"Watch out for Willow's hand, everyone," warned Delia's mom.

"Girls, we wanted to show you what we just found," Grandma was saying. "It's from one of the old photo albums I brought. We thought you might get a kick out of it."

And flipping open the scrapbook in her lap, Grandma held up one of the pages. An old black-and-white picture was taped there.

Delia pointed the flashlight at the image, and she and Willow pressed in close to see. Their moms on either side of them leaned in too, so now five sets of eyes were straining to get a glimpse of the photo. It was of a skinny girl with a triangle-shaped tent behind her.

"That's not you, is it, Grandma?" Willow asked.

"It is," Grandma said with a grin. "I was just about your age, girls."

Their moms pointed out Grandma's knobby knees and long hair. Grandma tapped at the lavender bush growing beside the tent. "I had a thing for flowers, even then." And they all laughed at the way her tent was held up by a rope strung between two trees.

But it was Delia who spotted the most exciting detail.

"Grandma, what's that you're wearing in the photo?" she asked. "I think that's the daisy necklace! Look, Willow, there it is!"

All five heads pressed together again, pushing in even closer to the old photo album. Delia adjusted the flashlight's beam so it hit just right. And sure enough, the faintest image of a necklace came into focus.

"That little daisy pendant meant the world to me," Grandma said, putting her arm first around Willow and then Delia. "I couldn't be happier to know it's getting a new life with one of my granddaughters."

And then, snapping her fingers as if she'd just re-membered something, Grandma picked the album up again and flipped through the pages. She stopped on another picture from her childhood. This time there was a woman with her, hands resting on Grandma's shoulders, hair stiff and teased high like a helmet.

"That's my mother," Grandma said. "And look on her finger there, Delia. It's your ring!"

This time, their heads pressed in so quickly, they knocked together like coconuts. Delia squinted hard at the photograph until she saw it. There on the hand resting on Grandma's shoulder was the very same ring: a thin band with a tiny emerald. Delia reached for her own finger. She twisted the ring around and around, feeling the connection from her hand

through her mom to her grandmother, and on to the lady in the photo—her great-grandmother.

"I'll take good care of it, Grandma," she promised, a few goose bumps breaking out on her arms. "I can see how special this ring is."

And as the wind rustled the trees, a few moon shadows danced across the yard. Delia's mom gave a nervous shudder and huddled in closer to Delia. Even though she was a nurse and dealt with gross things all the time. Delia's mom got the creeps pretty easily. Delia pointed out a bat that was flitting through the sky, its black silhouette clear against the moonlit night. That made her mom flinch and bury her head in Delia's shoulder.

Delia laughed, reminding her mom of all the good things about bats.

"Why don't we all sleep out here together?" she suggested. Since they'd moved to Saugatuck, her mom didn't have to work two jobs anymore, which meant she had more time for Delia—and for having fun. "We've never done a campout with Grandma."

"And we have enough extra blankets to go around," Willow said, springing to her knees.

Delia couldn't help but smile. Her cousin could still bounce with excitement, even when she was sitting down.

Grandma said there was nowhere she'd rather be than right here, camping with the girls. But what about her daughters?

"Deenie," began Grandma, her voice playfully scolding, "you aren't afraid to sleep out here in the dark, are you? I remember both you and Aggie as being brave when you were these girls' ages. That hasn't changed, has it?"

Delia's mom and Aunt Aggie said of course they weren't afraid. What was there to be afraid of? It's not like a bear was going to walk by, they said. Or raccoons. Or possums.

"Or wolverines," Delia added. "They're all common to our part of Michigan."

"Wolverines!" exclaimed her mom. "Do you mean a wolverine could be out here? Have you seen their teeth? They could hurt if they attack!"

"Don't be scared, Mom," Delia said, giving her mother's shoulder a comforting pat. "Willow, Grandma, and I will protect you."

This drew smiles and laughter and nudges back and forth. Though a call from the treetops made them fall silent.

It was the hooting of the rain owl. Maybe it was saying good night, Delia wondered. Or telling their moms not to be frightened.

"Did that owl just ask, *Who cooks for you?*" wondered Aunt Aggie. "I swear that's what it sounded like."

"You're right! That's how birders describe the rain owl's call," Delia explained. "I read about it in one of the books you sent me."

"Oh, no," Willow whispered, "you two aren't going to hold a book club right now, are you?" And she told Delia and her mom to hush.

The five eager campers went quiet again, listening to the wind whisper through the leaves and the waves wash against the shore. Crickets kept up their chirping, and the frogs whirred and croaked. Finally, the rain owl let out its questioning hoot again.

"Who cooks for you? Who cooks for you all?"

And Delia and Willow answered.

"We do!"

Chapter 6
shelter from the storm

The clock read 2:17 a.m. when Delia opened her eyes. It was the second time she'd been woken up already.

The first came a few hours ago, just before midnight, as rain was pelting the roof of the tent. Grandma had wanted to stay and ride out the downpour. But Delia's mom and Aunt Deenie had ordered everybody inside to their own beds.

Now, it was a crash of thunder that made Delia nearly jump out of her covers. She was upstairs at Whispering Pines in the room she always shared with Willow, rather than in her bedroom next door.

And as lightning lit up the sky outside the windows, she saw that Sweet William was in their room too. He was standing beside Willow's bed and trying to shake her awake.

"Come on, Willow, get up," he whispered, though his attempts at being quiet were failing. "It's Bernice—she needs you. And Gossie too!"

"I'm awake, Sweet William," Delia called, slipping over to Willow's bed. "What's the matter? Are

Bernice and Gossie hurt? Are they lost?"

Finally, Willow began to stir, pushing up onto her elbows to listen.

"It's the thunder," he began. "It makes Bernice crazy. She's so scared, she hasn't stopped shaking for hours. She's curled up tight under the kitchen table whimpering. And Gossie's outside! I couldn't get him to come in and stay with us. He's out there in the garden somewhere!"

Delia reached to the nightstand beside her and grabbed the yellow flashlight she'd had in the tent, along with her first-aid kit. She liked being ready with a bandage in case anyone—cousin, canine, or Canada goose—might need one. Willow groggily got to her feet, and the threesome slipped down the stairs to the kitchen to find Bernice.

"It's okay, girl," soothed Willow, trying to coax the hundred-and-seventeen-pound bundle of nerves out from beneath the table. She tried peanut butter on a spoon, then cheese squares. What they really needed was Bernice's favorite: bacon. That's the only thing that could make their dog budge in this storm.

"We've got to find Gossie," Sweet William said, his forehead crinkled with worry. "The wind might blow him away. And the thundercats are scary."

Delia looked at Willow and scratched her head. *Thundercats?*

"Do you mean thunder*claps?*" she wondered, slipping the first-aid kit into her pajama pocket. "That's the sound thunder makes as it crashes around in the sky."

"Well, cats are really scary, too," he said, his eyes welling up, "especially if you're a bird sitting outside in the dark, without your mom or your dog." And now Sweet William looked as if he might really start crying.

"It's all right," said Willow, putting her hand on her little brother's shoulder. "We can go out there and look for Gossie. We'll bring him back in here, and he can sleep under the table with Bernice. Okay?"

Sweet William let out a sniffle that both girls took for an okay. Putting Sweet William between them, they each held one of his hands and pushed open the back door.

The wind was fierce, and Delia reached for the porch railing to hold on to so she wasn't blown backward into the door. Sweet William and Willow pressed in close to Delia, and they eased themselves down the steps, leaning into the wind. Delia led the way, her yellow flashlight's beam shining into the black night.

The rain stung their faces.

"He was in the garden before," Sweet William shouted over the gusts. "We can check there first!"

The three cousins skirted along the edge of the house as they rounded the backyard and headed for Cat's garden. The tomato vines and pepper plants were pressed over, bent nearly to the ground by the strong winds off Lake Michigan. Delia wasn't sure how smart it was to be outside on a night like this, especially with lightning slicing through the sky. But the thought of Gossie out here alone made her push on.

They clung tightly to each other as they dashed up the garden row, the mud squishing between their toes. Lettuce plants and all sorts of vegetable vines brushed against them as they shuffled along, Delia's flashlight catching the heavy rain in its beam.

"I see something white over there!" Delia hollered. And when she pointed the flashlight to the far corner of the garden, they saw him. Gossie. He was lying nearly flat to the ground at the base of an enormous broccoli bush. "We'll have to carry him back!"

Willow nodded, her face dripping. "I hope he's not hurt."

"I hope he doesn't bite us the way Mother Goose did last summer!" Sweet William shouted. "That hurt pretty bad."

When they reached Gossie, it was clear he was miserable. His feathers were plastered down, his beak buried in his wing. He looked exhausted. Sweet William pulled a handful of grain from his pajama pocket and offered it. But the rain quickly washed it out of his palm.

"What's that?" he shouted as Gossie flapped and flailed in Willow's arms. The goose seemed to be putting up a good fight as Willow tried to tuck him under her arm, ignoring her bandaged fingers. Sweet William was pointing at a round white ball that was under Gossie's feathers.

"It's an egg!" shouted Willow. "Sweet William, I think Gossie's a she-goose, not a he-goose!"

Delia picked up the egg and turned it gingerly in her hands. And then she noticed two more, just like the first one.

"And Gossie's not having one gosling," Delia said, handing her flashlight to Sweet William to hold. She cradled the first egg gently in her pajama shirt. Then, reaching under the lowest leaves of the broccoli plant, Delia picked up the other two. She stood up just as another bolt of lightning crackled through the sky over the water. "Gossie's having triplets! Let's hurry back inside and get these geese—and ourselves—somewhere safer!"

And as they headed down the garden row again, each of them carefully carrying a delicate load, Delia could hear Willow talking to herself. "Three more baby geese? Mom is not going to be happy about this news!"

It wasn't too much later when a cardboard box was located, dry towels spread inside, and Gossie and her three eggs were tucked in for the night. Since Bernice wouldn't get out from under the table, Gossie's box was slipped underneath too. Though Bernice was too nervous to sniff inside, her wagging tail let them know that she approved.

And with Bernice and Gossie tucked under the kitchen table, Sweet William wouldn't sleep anywhere else. "What kind of friend do you think I am?" he whisper-shouted.

So Willow and Delia headed upstairs to peel out of their wet clothes for the second time and change into fresh, dry ones. Delia helped Willow replace her bandage again, delicately wrapping dry gauze around the splint that protected her cousin's bruised fingers. They were careful not to wake anyone in the nearby rooms.

Delia tiptoed into her little cousin's room and poked around until she found a pair of his pajamas, along with his blanket and pillow, and another dry towel.

"It's after three in the morning," she whispered as they slinked around their own bedroom. "I could fall asleep standing up!"

Both cousins quickly pulled blankets from closets and rounded up more pillows, then returned to the kitchen. They pitched a second campsite, this time with Sweet William and his furry and feathered friends instead of with Grandma and their mothers.

"I always wanted to have a morning adventure with you guys," Sweet William said once he was out of his wet clothes. He curled up beside Bernice beneath the table, happily tucking into his favorite blanket.

Lightning lit up the entire kitchen and was quickly followed by a clap of thunder that rattled the walls. "You're right about those thunder*cats*, Sweet William," Delia whispered. "It's raining cats and dogs out there right now."

"Or as Grandpa would say, it's raining cat's-paws and dogwoods," Willow chuckled from her pillow. "Get it? Those are flowers."

But Sweet William didn't need any explaining. He was already asleep.

Chapter 7
thursday's alarming start

delia was dreaming about a furry caterpillar tickling her nose when she woke up the next morning. She blinked a few moments in the pale light. Her eyes were fixed on the long black-and-white caterpillar-looking thing on her pillow.

"Willow?" she whispered curiously. "What is this?"

At the sound of Delia's voice, the furry black caterpillar began to wag. And that's when Delia saw it was connected to a dog. Bernice, that is, who was delighted to have so much company after such a frightening night. Bernice scooted around to face her wakeful friend, licking Delia's forehead and ear in a grateful sunrise greeting.

"Good morning," Delia whispered back, scratching Bernice's floppy ears. "I remember where we are now. Camping out with you, Gossie, and Sweet William."

As Delia slid out from under the table, she reached over Sweet William's sleeping body to Willow's. She poked her cousin in the arm a few times until, finally, Willow started to wake up.

"Rise and shine, Sleeping Beauty," Delia called softly. "Let's have some breakfast. And then we can figure out what to make for Aunt Rosie's shower—she eats a lot since she's so hugely pregnant. We should make her favorite things."

Willow sat up with a start, knocking her head into the table. "Ouch!" she groaned. "And yuck. It's so creepy thinking about Aunt Rosie's giant belly this early in the morning." She rubbed her forehead, looking around. "Where are we?"

"Under the kitchen table," Delia reminded in

a whisper, shushing Willow not to wake Sweet William. "Remember? The rain sent us inside from the tent. Then Bernice and Gossie were scared of the thunderstorm. So we slept in the kitchen."

Willow started to rise from her pillow, only to smack her head again. Delia covered her mouth so her cousin wouldn't see her laughing.

"I love everything about the kitchen here at Whispering Pines," Willow croaked softly, scratching her tangle of curls. "But I don't know how much I love sleeping on the kitchen floor. It's really hard."

Delia got up and rummaged around for a frying pan, then she pulled out a carton of eggs from the refrigerator. "We can cook up those raspberries to make a jam, too," she said, pointing toward a bright bowl on the white countertop. "I picked a whole pail and brought them over here before you came. The hummingbirds led me to them."

Willow found a loaf of bread and popped two slices into the toaster. She rubbed her tender fingers and her sore head, then she yawned. They both agreed that fried eggs with toast and raspberry jam sounded delicious.

"Those hummingbirds are still bringing good luck," Willow said, popping a red berry into her mouth. "Have you ever heard that good luck comes in threes? That if one good thing happens, it's usually followed by two more good things?"

Delia cracked an egg onto the big pan as Willow added sugar to the raspberries in the smaller one.

"I've only heard that *bad* luck comes in threes," Delia said. "Like the time I lost a tooth and couldn't play in my flute recital. And that same day, my flip-flops melted on the hot sidewalk. And the next day, a penguin sneezed on my head at zoo camp. That's the kind of bad-luck threes I know about."

Willow said she hoped their vacation was off to a lucky start. "Our third lucky thing will be getting to help with Aunt Rosie's baby shower on Saturday."

"Sure, but what are the first two?" Delia wanted to know. "How can the baby shower be our third good-luck thing when we don't even know what the first and second things are?"

"Maybe it's winning a County Fair contest," Willow said. "Or finally getting the kitchen all to ourselves—like right now. Let's decide on a recipe!"

So as they sat down to their breakfast, the cousins grabbed Willow's polka-dotted bag from the far corner of the kitchen and flipped open the tattered recipe notebook that was tucked inside. Delia was glad to hear Willow mention the contest along with the baby shower. She still wanted to tell her more about

plan, but when? And would there be enough time to do all that baking?

After a bit of back-and-forth in between bites, they reached an agreement on what recipe to make first. "Angel food cake," they said at the same time. Maybe it was the photo of a baby with angel wings hovering over a cake that did the trick. But it seemed like the perfect thing to serve Aunt Rosie at her shower.

Delia began pulling down the sugar, the salt, the flour, and the vanilla, and she watched her cousin open up the container of eggs and start cracking— one-handed, of course. Delia couldn't help but smile. Willow was amazing

Just as they were ready to pour their batter into a baking pan, Sweet William slid out from under the table and announced he was hungry. So Delia set down the mixing bowl and pulled out a fresh plate, and Willow loaded it up with the rest of the fried eggs and a slice of bread with jam. They were happy he was joining them *at* the table instead of hiding *under* it.

"What's that noise?" he asked after a few minutes of sleepy chewing. Bread crumbs clung to his lips as he tilted his head to hear.

"Did Mr. Henry get a louder alarm clock?" asked Willow, giving the cake batter another stir.

"I don't think that's an alarm clock," said Delia. She set down the baking pan and stepped toward the screen door. "That's a fire alarm! And it sounds like it's coming from my house!"

Sweet William's fork dropped onto his plate in a noisy clatter. And Delia and Willow left their batter behind as they raced out of the kitchen, down the back porch steps, and toward the yellow house. They passed the soggy tent, the grass still wet under their bare feet.

"Is that smoke?" hollered Willow, pointing at one of the downstairs windows.

"Girls, stay back," shouted Uncle Liam. He and Aunt Aggie had just emerged from the front door of Whispering Pines, their bathrobes flapping behind them as they ran.

"If you folks don't mind waiting here, where it's safe," began Mr. Henry in his calm manner. He was already on the brick path leading to the café's front steps. "I will proceed inside to find Ms. Catherine and your family, Delia." His white hair was standing on end, and Delia realized she'd never seen him go anywhere without his sun hat.

Just the sight of Mr. Henry looking slightly off made Delia suddenly feel unsettled. Her worries about having to leave the cheery yellow house came rushing into her mind. But instead of losing it to slow business, were they going to lose it to a fire?

"We've got to help!" she shouted, trying to follow Mr. Henry up the café steps. But Willow grabbed her shoulder and begged her to stay put.

"I've already called 9-1-1," announced Aunt Aggie, wrapping her arms around all three of the cousins. "The fire trucks should be here any minute. Don't worry!"

Suddenly the kitchen window opened wide, and Cat waved a flowery dish towel out into the yard.

"Everybody's all right, y'all," she called. "It's just some cookies"—*cough, cough*—"got a little over-cooked"—*cough, cough*—"and they set off the"—*gasp*—"smoke detectors."

Everyone in the yard heaved a sigh of relief. And it was only a few minutes later when Cat pushed open the yellow screen door and came down the café's front steps. She didn't look scared about the fire alarm. But with her red cheeks and angry eyes, Cat looked like she was still pretty hot.

Next out the door, to Delia's great relief, was her family.

"We didn't mean for the cookies to burn," Darlene was saying, rushing behind Delia's mom and dad, her arms gesturing wildly. "We were only trying to bake a dessert!"

"To sell at the café," added Violet, a little flour smudged on her cheek. "They were going to be amazing cookies! We threw about six different things into the batter. Only I guess we should have set the oven to 'Bake' instead of 'Broil.'"

Delia threw her arms around her mom, her dad, and Darlene, grateful everyone was okay. And she gave an affectionate pat to the wooden Arts & Eats Café sign too. What a relief that the place was unharmed.

Once everybody was safely outside, Mr. Henry said he was going back in to double-check the kitchen. He wanted to make sure those smoking cookies weren't starting a real fire.

That's when sirens pierced the morning.

"Fire trucks are here," cheered Sweet William, running in circles with Bernice at his heels. "Maybe they'll rescue the cookies and find Cat's patience."

Willow looked confused. And Delia raised an eyebrow in Sweet William's direction.

"What do you mean?" she asked her little cousin.

Sweet William waved excitedly at the firefighters as they ran up the café's steps and into Arts & Eats.

"Cat said she'd lost her patience with Darlene and Violet in her kitchen," Sweet William explained. "I think the firefighters can help find it, don't you?"

Six-Kinds-of-Wonderful Cookies

Ingredients:

2 cups flour
1 teaspoon baking soda
½ cup (1 stick) butter, softened
1 cup brown sugar
2 eggs

1 teaspoon vanilla
2 cups oats
1 cup raisins
1 cup dried cranberries
1 cup chocolate chips
1 cup M&M'S
1 cup peanut butter

Directions:

1. Make sure you have an adult's help.

2. Heat oven to 350 degrees.

3. Pour the dry ingredients—flour and baking soda—in a bowl.

4. In a larger bowl, use a fork to mix the butter with brown sugar until it is creamy. Then add the eggs and vanilla. Combine the dry ingredients in with the creamy.

5. Add in your special ingredients—the oats, raisins, dried cranberries, chocolate chips, M&M'S, and peanut butter. Mix it all together.

6. Using a ¼-cup measure, drop the dough onto a cookie sheet covered with parchment paper.

7. Bake for about 12 minutes or until golden brown. But pay attention not to burn the cookies!

Makes about 2 dozen cookies.

Chapter 8
"i want to ask a favor of y'all"

When the fire trucks pulled away and the rest of the family started shuffling back indoors—in search of coffee and showers and a bit more sleep—Cat pulled Delia and Willow aside.

"I need to talk to y'all," she said, patting her wavy-macaroni hair distractedly. "I'm sure those big sisters of yours are sweet as sugar lumps," she began. Willow let out a snort. "But when they get in my kitchen, I'm like a long-tailed cat in a room full of rockin' chairs." And with Cat's drawl, it sounded more like *chay-yers*. "They get me so nervous when they try to cook something. The two of them are making me twitchy."

Cat put a hand on each of their shoulders, as if she needed the cousins' support to help her cross the lawn. And together they walked along Grandma's new stone path as it wound its way from the café toward Whispering Pines.

"First it was the overflowing oatmeal," Cat began. "Then came the brownie-batter splatter—I found some of it speckled onto my window and curtains!" She pushed her cat's-eye glasses up on her nose, taking a deep breath. "And now this, cookie baking that calls the fire department."

Delia leaned past Cat and caught Willow's eye, giving her cousin a knowing look. *Bad-luck threes*, she mouthed. Willow nodded back.

Cat said she didn't have time for any more trouble in her kitchen. She'd just gotten a call from her friend, the one who was going to bake the cake for Aunt Rosie's baby shower.

"She came down with a bad case of poison ivy, and the last thing she wants is to make anyone else itchy," Cat said with a sigh. "So there you have it. She can't help with Rosie's shower. Now it's back to me."

Delia gave Willow a look. She wanted her cousin to speak up, to tell Cat they could bake the desserts for Aunt Rosie's baby shower.

Willow gave her a look right back. She seemed too nervous to speak.

But before either could pipe up, Cat was talking again.

"Saturday is coming at us fast, y'all. There's Aunt Rosie's baby shower to think about, not to mention that pickling contest at the County Fair," she said, her steps slowing as they talked. "And I'm behind Henry Rickles and his pickles one hundred percent. We've got a good chance of winning a blue ribbon. And like Henry said, that's just the thing the Arts and Eats Café needs. It's sure to win us some customers!"

Willow told Cat she was sure Mr. Henry would take first prize. But Delia tugged nervously at her braid.

What if Mr. Henry didn't win?

What would happen to Cat's café then?

What would happen to her dad and his paintings? And to living here in Saugatuck?

"So I want to ask a favor of y'all," Cat said once they reached the back porch at Whispering Pines. She bent lower so she was looking into their faces. "I'm busy as a squirrel in a nuthouse this week. I'm working as hard as I can with Mr. Henry on those pickles. And I've got to make a new batch of desserts—to sell at the café and to serve at the baby shower."

Delia reached over and squeezed Willow's good hand.

Willow squeezed right back.

Because it seemed like a good-luck moment was happening right before their amber eyes. Cat was about to ask them to help with all the baking, Delia just knew it. Willow was going to be so happy!

"What I want to ask you is this," Cat said, her eyes lingering on Willow's injured hand. "Do y'all think you can keep those sisters of yours out of my café's kitchen?"

Chapter 9
baby-belly talk

The cousins trudged up the porch steps toward the kitchen. Willow looked stunned, and Delia was still replaying Cat's words through her head. *Keep those sisters of yours out of my café's kitchen?*

"Why didn't she ask *us* to make the desserts?" said Willow, her face bewildered as she adjusted the gauze on her pinkie finger. "Weren't we amazing last summer?"

Delia assured her they were. "Maybe she thinks we're too young. Or that we just want to play on the beach this year." She shrugged, making sure not to mention Willow's hand. "Or she doesn't want to ask us because it might hurt our sisters' feelings."

"It's all right," Willow said, her eyes determined again. "We'll show everybody. Let's get back to our angel food cake."

Thwack!

The screen door slammed behind them as they stepped into the kitchen. But there was no angel food cake waiting for them. No batter, no sacks of flour or sugar, no eggs or vanilla. The white countertops were wiped clean. And the mixing bowl and cake pan were washed and drying on the rack.

"What happened in here?" asked Delia, trying hard to keep her voice calm.

Aunt Rosie turned around from the refrigerator, a hunk of bright orange cheese in one hand, sliced ham in the other. Their mothers were at the wooden stools around the island, finishing off the toast and raspberry jam.

"Grandpa was cleaning up when we came in," Rosie said, gesturing with the cheese. "And I just wanted a little nibble to tide me over."

"Your aunt Rosie is a bit hungry these days," began Delia's mom, whose mouth was so full of toast, her words came out a little puffy. "You know, when a baby grows in a mother's tummy . . ."

"*Eeew!*" Willow covered her ears and squeezed her eyes shut.

"We're helping her get enough food," added Aunt Aggie, licking the last remnants of jam off the spoon. "She's eating for two now."

"At least," sighed Aunt Rosie as she gingerly edged onto one of the stools. "But there are things I can't eat, like raw honey and sushi. And what I miss most of all: coffee. I'm allowed to have a cup or so. But the rest of that stuff isn't so good for the baby."

Aunt Rosie rubbed her beach-ball belly and said

something about the baby kicking. This sent Aunt Aggie and Delia's mom into squeals of delight.

"*Eeew* again," Willow whispered, though only Delia seemed to have heard it.

Delia nudged her squeamish cousin with her shoulder. All this baby talk was a good distraction from the worries of the morning. But still, the knot in Delia's stomach was helping her keep track: the fire alarm over at the yellow house, Cat wanting them to keep their sisters out of her kitchen, and now the missing cake batter.

With the County Fair contest tomorrow and the baby shower the next day, how would she and Willow ever get anything baked in time?

"I can't wait to see what desserts Cat is making for the shower," said Aunt Rosie between bites of ham and cheese. "Did you girls know we're going with a yellow theme for the party? No blue-is-for-boys, pink-is-for-girls stuff, since we won't reveal any secrets about your new cousin."

Delia was relieved to hear it. After last summer's

periwinkle-blue wedding shower that matched Jonathan's eyes, she was afraid a yellow party was supposed to match the color of his hair. She shot a look over at Willow. But her cousin was staring at Rosie's enormous stomach and looking completely baffled.

Aunt Aggie pulled a pencil from her bun and started making one of her lists.

"First, here are some reminders for you and your sister, Willow," she began. "When you see Violet, make sure to tell her she needs to practice for her ukulele recital. It's coming up in July. And you need to pull your violin out of the car too. Both of you should be practicing twenty minutes a day. Even on vacation!"

Willow's shoulders sagged a little more. And Delia started to wonder whether her cousin was in the middle of bad-luck threes.

Aunt Aggie tore the page out of her notebook and handed it to Willow. Then she began a new list.

"Here are a few yellow dessert ideas for Cat," she said, and her two sisters leaned in close to offer advice. "With all this rain, maybe a yellow-themed party will bring out the sunshine." And her pencil flew across the paper as she wrote.

"Don't forget lemon bars," Delia's mom said, tapping the paper.

"And bananas," added Aunt Rosie, craning her neck to read her sister's handwriting. "I've been craving bananas for weeks."

"And sugar cookies with lemon icing," Aunt Aggie said. "Maybe even something with yellow marshmallows. Cat could shape them like baby birds."

Finally, with a quick *rip*, they tore the paper from the notepad and laid it on the counter with instructions to show it to Cat.

Delia caught Willow's eye. She lifted her eyebrow just a bit, asking a silent question. Willow gave a quick nod in response.

And in that instant, another deal was sealed.

Like so many of their other unspoken agreements, the cousins didn't have to utter a single word. With that quick glance, they both knew exactly who would be making lemon-yellow desserts for Aunt Rosie's baby shower.

And it was going to be a delicious secret.

"Cat loves lemons," Delia said, turning the ring on her finger for good luck.

"And yellow desserts are a great idea," Willow agreed, picking up her mom's note.

With three quick good-byes, kisses blowing through the hot summer air toward Delia and Willow, the three Bumpus sisters were gone.

Thwack! Thwack! Thwack!

"Their suggestions are pretty good," Willow began, grabbing her tattered recipe folder again. "But that County Fair contest is coming up. Do you think we can do it all?"

Delia turned to Willow and her injured hand, taking a moment to smooth down the white gauze where it was bunching up. Nobody else seemed to think they could do much this summer, but Delia didn't want that to stop them. She couldn't wait to get started.

"Today is Thursday," Delia began, feeling that fizzy excitement again. "The County Fair contest is tomorrow, and the baby shower isn't until Saturday. So that means . . . there's plenty of time!"

"I'll grab the measuring spoons," Willow said with a broad grin.

But before they got too far, Sweet William pushed open the door from the dining room. He was wearing swim goggles over his eyes. And a snorkel made his breathing loud and raspy.

"What are you doing, Sweet William?" asked Willow. "Can you breathe with that thing? You sound like Darth Vader."

"I'm getting ready for Aunt Rosie's shower," he explained, pulling the snorkel mouthpiece from his lips. "I don't like when water gets in my eyes."

And with awkward steps—he was wearing long yellow flippers on his feet and red floaties on his arms—he picked up Gossie's cardboard box and flapped out of the kitchen. Bernice followed behind him, but she kept her distance from his noisy feet.

Grandma was next to come through the kitchen, moments after Sweet William. She poured herself a cup of coffee, though her bright green gardening gloves made it hard to hold the mug. Then she peered out the window over the sink and said something about getting to work before the rain came.

"If you see your uncles," she said, picking up a flowery umbrella and resting it on her shoulder like she was a soldier marching into battle, "send them out to find me. There's more work to be done to get this yard ready for a party."

And as the screen door *thwack*ed behind Grandma, Delia thought she heard the door to the dining room *whoosh* shut. She and Willow crossed the kitchen and pushed it open, peeking into the room. The uncles were standing there, fingers pressed to their lips to keep the girls quiet.

"Please don't tell Grandma you saw us," Uncle Jonathan begged. "My back is killing me!"

"We just need a few more minutes to relax," whispered Uncle Liam, clutching his empty coffee cup.

"She made us carry all that mulch yesterday," moaned Delia's dad. "My arms are aching."

After refilling the three coffee mugs, Willow and Delia went back to their recipe notebook. But the rustling of a newspaper page made them both jump. It was Grandpa, sitting at the far corner of the kitchen table and quietly reading. Delia had forgotten he was even there.

"Grandpa, why aren't you in the yard helping Grandma with the landscaping?" asked Willow. "You've got all those years from the flower shop. Don't you want to help plant begonias?"

Grandpa folded his paper and looked out the open windows. The sounds of Sweet William's laughter and Bernice's barking drifted in with the breeze.

"Here's a joke for this morning. Why is a big dog like a tree?" he asked, taking a sip of his coffee and waiting a beat or two. "They both have a lot of bark."

Delia and Willow smiled, but Grandpa wrinkled his eyebrows.

"I'd say Grandma has got a lot of bark these days

about that garden," he said with a huff. "I'd rather keep out of it."

Delia told him he was welcome to stay with them in the Whispering Pines kitchen. She and Willow were planning to bake for most of the day. "And after that visit from the fire department, it's probably good to have a grown-up nearby to check the oven," Delia said.

"Sensible girl," Grandpa replied. Then he added, "I apologize for dumping out your cake batter. I know you two are quite good with a whisk. But with all that commotion next door, well, I didn't want you girls getting into the same sort of trouble as your sisters."

Delia stepped over and planted a quick kiss on the top of Grandpa's head. Willow wrapped her arms around his shoulders, saying it was no big deal. "You probably saved us"—she grinned—"because we need to bake yellow desserts, not white."

Now Grandma's voice could be heard coming through the open window. "Jonathan! Liam! Delvan!

I see you three hiding behind that tree. Come on over here and help move these stones!"

Grandpa chuckled and opened up his newspaper again, mumbling something about Grandma being like a fire-breathing snapdragon. He told Delia and Willow he'd be nearby if they needed him.

Chapter 10
does might make right?

"So first we make a lemon cake," Willow suggested, finally getting back to the mixing bowls. "Those are easy. Then we can move on to sugar cookies with lemon icing. And I've got a few more lemony recipes in my notebook."

Delia thumbed through the notebook and felt her mouth water from the delicious-looking photographs Willow had taped there. "After that, we can do something with bananas. And finally, we can finish with crepes or pudding or something else that's yellow."

"Crepes? Pudding?" said Willow, her eyes bulging as if Delia had just walked out of a spaceship.

"What about cupcakes?"

"I do want to make cupcakes, Willow," she began. "I want to make amazing cupcakes! But let's enter them in the County Fair contest—just like Mr. Henry. Only we wouldn't be competing for prize pickling, the way he is. We would compete to win a blue ribbon in the Cakes and Cupcakes Contest!"

Willow fiddled with a measuring spoon, as if she were giving Delia's plan a good long think. "Cupcakes are what we do best," Willow said thoughtfully, "so it seems like they should be for the baby shower. Why are you so focused on the County Fair contest instead of Aunt Rosie's party? What's the big deal?"

"Don't you see, Willow? This is exactly how we can help the café," Delia began. "You heard Cat and Mr. Henry. If they win a blue ribbon at the fair for their pickles, the whole town will know about it. And more people will come out to the Arts and Eats Café to taste them."

"And if more people come," Willow said, picking up Delia's train of thought, "then business will be good—both for Cat and for your dad. And then your family can keep on living at the yellow house."

Delia sighed, grateful Willow understood her plan. But the knot in her stomach tightened again. Could they really do this? Especially with Willow's hurt hand? They were just a couple of kids.

But still, Delia reminded herself, *a couple of kids* saved the wedding last summer.

Willow picked up a silver whisk, waving it slowly in the air like a magic wand. "I still imagine being a

chef when I grow up," Willow teased, "but Delia, I think you dream of being a fairy godmother."

Delia smiled. Being a fairy godmother didn't sound like a bad job—she'd always wanted to have fairy wings. And she always wanted to make sure her family was happy too.

Delia was willing to use everything she could—even a magic whisk—to make it happen.

"So what kind of cupcakes should we bake?" Willow was asking. "Peanut-butter-and-jelly ones? Carrot-cake cupcakes?"

Delia said she'd been thinking hard about it too. They needed to make something that was delicious but unusual, tasty but clever.

"What if," Delia began, "we baked our cupcakes in ice-cream cones? And we made the frosting look like ice cream?"

She held her breath, waiting for Willow's response. Did she hate the idea? Delia looked into her cousin's face and tried to read her expression.

Finally, Willow broke into a broad grin. "I love

it!" she said. "We can top each one with sprinkles and a cherry from Grandma's tree," she said, her curls like springs on her shoulders. "Because nothing can beat rainbow sprinkles and a cherry on top!"

It was a few hours later, just after lunchtime, when the screen door let them know they had visitors again.

Thwack!

Sweet William stepped in with a nervous-looking Bernice beside him. Gossie and her eggs were riding in the cardboard box he carried in his arms. A low rumble of thunder echoed from somewhere far over the lake.

"Bernice and me really don't like thunder," he said, setting the box beside the kitchen table and moving a few chairs out of the way. Bernice was burrowing as far under the table as she could get. "It makes my teeth chatter. And it makes Bernice a nervous rug."

"I don't think you mean *rug*," corrected Delia as she peeked beneath the table at him. "You probably mean nervous *wreck*."

"Sure I do," Sweet William said, wiping at his nose. Then he scooted his box and his bottom closer toward Bernice. "Just watch Bernice. Whenever she hears thunder, she lies down under the kitchen table just like a rug. There's no safer place to be, if you ask me."

The cousins were just getting back to their mixing when another *thwack! thwack!* from the screen door let them know more visitors were coming in.

"What are you guys doing over here?" asked Darlene. She and Violet were looking around at the messy countertops crowded with bags of flour and sugar, mixing bowls of various sizes, and lots of measuring cups and spoons.

"Nothing!" shouted Willow and Delia at the same time.

That didn't quite convince their big sisters.

"You can't possibly be baking," said Darlene, gesturing toward Willow's bandaged hand.

"Whatever you're doing," ordered Violet as she tried not to touch any of the broken eggshells, "you have to clear out, because we have things we

want to do in here."

Willow's eyes squeezed shut, and she looked as if she were about to start yelling. That's when Delia snatched up the list from Aunt Aggie and handed it to their big sisters.

"Your mom wanted us to remind you, Violet," Delia began, trying to make her voice calm. "She says you're supposed to practice your ukulele. A lot. Today. *Now!* At least, that's what she said."

"And Darlene is supposed to help you," added

Willow. "You know, sing along and all that."

Both Violet and Darlene folded their arms across their chests. They didn't seem to believe their little sisters.

"Practice the ukulele on vacation?" Violet demanded. "Are you serious?"

Delia pointed at the slip of paper from Aunt Aggie's notebook as evidence.

"With the baby shower coming up . . ." Willow began, and Delia noticed a few splotches of pink on her cousin's neck. Willow always got splotchy when she was angry. Or nervous. Or happy. "Well . . . um . . . they *might* need you guys to play for Aunt Rosie. You know, make her baby shower really special. Because you guys are both so . . ."

And here Willow paused for what felt to Delia like an eternity.

". . . good," Delia finally said.

She wasn't exactly sure what she and Willow were doing. But if they didn't hurry up and shoo their big sisters out of the kitchen, they wouldn't get anything done in time for the shower. Or the County Fair contest.

"B-but it should be a big secret," Delia stammered, trying to come up with something to say. "So don't go around talking about it to anyone. Just, you know, get the song right. For Aunt Rosie's sake."

Darlene turned to Violet. "Are you ready to play in front of an audience? That might take more courage than I have."

Violet waved her off with a confident smile. "No problem, Darlene," she said. "It's not really an *audience*. It's just family. Let's go practice!"

The screen door smacked behind them as Violet and Darlene shot out of the kitchen, barely saying good-bye as they headed off for the yellow house and Violet's ukulele.

And two hands smacked two foreheads as Willow and Delia considered what they'd just done.

"We had to get rid of them if we want to get all this baking done!" said Willow, looking a little guilty.

"I know, but did we have to lie?" worried Delia.

Willow said it wasn't exactly a lie. She hadn't told their sisters that Jonathan and their moms had *asked* them to perform at the shower. "I said they *might* need Darlene and Violet to play. That's different!"

There was a rustling of newspaper from the corner, and Grandpa spoke up.

"I'd say *might* is a mighty good word sometimes," he said, tucking his newspaper under one arm and heading for the porch. "Because what you girls just did *might* have been just what your sisters needed."

Chapter 11
kitchen construction zone

With the kitchen mostly to themselves again—the latest thunder had sent a furry dog, a nesting goose, and a fretful little brother even farther underneath the table—Delia and Willow returned to their baking. And soon a sunny, citrus aroma filled the room. The lemon cake was waiting to be frosted, and they were just pulling the lemon cookies from the oven to cool on the back counter. The ice-cream-cone cupcakes were already finished, and now it was time to think about fruit tarts.

Delia washed the cherries, while Willow began pitting them.

But with every clap of thunder, the trio under the kitchen table began to tremble.

"Willow, I don't like this," Sweet William complained. "I'm afraid the lightning is going to hit the roof. And the thunder sounds like we're at a bowling alley."

Willow was lining up the ingredients on the countertop. She bent down with her mixing spoon in her good hand and tried to ease Sweet William's mind. "I

think thunder is exactly like a bowling alley," she explained. "It's just the clouds up there knocking down pins. Storms are kind of fun that way."

Sweet William said he didn't see anything fun about it.

Just then, Grandpa came back inside from the porch, pulling the newspaper from under his arm with a huff. He said he'd had enough of Grandma barking orders and making all the decisions. "She even chased me off—called me an old hollyhock. Of all things!"

He said he was hoping for a glass of fresh lemonade and a game of checkers. But Sweet William still wasn't so sure about coming out from under the table.

"Delia, what if we saved some of this baking for another time?" whispered Willow. "I think Grandpa and Sweet William could use a little help."

Delia agreed. Their cupcakes were ready for tomorrow's contest. And they could spend the rest of the day tomorrow making more things for Aunt Rosie's shower.

"Where is Sweet William's modeling clay?" Delia asked, hoping to coax her little cousin out from under the table with his favorite activity. "Maybe he could make the Clay Family and the Twig People like he did last summer."

Willow shook her head, saying the clay was too gloopy to use in all this heat. "And I haven't seen any fondant around the kitchen for him to roll into shapes. I wish I'd packed some Mentos or Good & Plenty candies like last summer."

Delia said Grandpa had a secret stash of gumdrops and jelly beans left over from Easter. The cousins peeked under the table at Sweet William and Bernice, and Gossie, too. Then their eyes went back up to Grandpa and his lonely expression as he sat at the kitchen table. They needed to find a project—and fast.

Speaking softly, Delia and Willow ran through a list of possibilities. What if they made rice-cereal treats and cut them into building blocks? Sugar cookies shaped like cars and trucks? Gingerbread men for waging battles?

"I've got it," said Willow with a grin. "What if we made gingerbread cookies, like we do at Christmas? Then Sweet William and Grandpa could build gingerbread houses. A construction project would keep them busy, don't you think?"

"Only instead of a Christmas house," Delia said, "they could build a summer beach house like Whispering Pines. And our yellow house next door."

In short order, gingerbread cookies were baking in the oven. The cousins had mixed and rolled and shaped and cut. And now they watched as the dough transformed into cookie triangles, rectangles, and squares perfect for building.

The mouthwatering promise of gingerbread, combined with the cozy feel the kitchen was giving off, eventually made Sweet William want to stretch his legs.

"The smell in here is *irritable!*" he announced, sniffing the air and shuffling over to the oven. "I can't wait to take a bite."

"Do you mean *irresistible?*" corrected Delia,

running her hand through Sweet William's loopy curls. "As in, you can't *resist* the smell of these cookies? Because *irritable* means you're quick to get annoyed."

"Well, I'll be *irritable* in a minute if I don't hurry up and get some gingerbread!" And he slipped into a chair beside Grandpa.

The two of them began their game of checkers as Willow and Delia got busy mixing up a bowl of white frosting. Delia wanted to make it just the right consistency to hold the gingerbread walls together.

"What kind of flower goes best with cookies?" asked Grandpa, shooting a wink over at Delia and Willow. And when they said they didn't know, he got up and headed for the refrigerator.

"Milkweed," he said, holding a gallon jug in his hand.

Sweet William slapped his knee and laughed, and Grandpa poured glasses of milk for them to share.

With the rest of her family appearing so relaxed, Bernice crept out from beneath the table too.

Stretching first her front legs, then her back ones, she sniffed her way around the baseboards of the entire room. Finally, once Willow assured her that the thunder had passed, she wandered over to her bowls of kibble and water.

Even Gossie hopped out of her box and waddled around the room, leaving her eggs to rest comfortably on the fluffy towels. And as the first big drops of rain began to fall, the residents of the Whispering Pines kitchen were blissfully unaware. There was construction work to be done, and the light of the cozy kitchen shone out into the dark and stormy night until well past ten o'clock.

Chapter 12
friday morning surprise

The next morning, the girls awoke to a low rumble that took them both a few minutes to figure out. It wasn't thunder rolling across the water toward Whispering Pines. It wasn't wind blowing through the trees and creaking the high branches. It wasn't Lake Michigan waves pounding the beach outside their window.

That rumbling was snoring. And it came from a human-size dog, an exhausted goose, and a slumbering little brother. At bedtime last night, the trio had felt brave enough to finally leave their hidey-hole in the kitchen and venture upstairs. But sleeping in

Sweet William's room—all alone—was out of the question. So Willow and Delia had agreed to let them camp out in the room they shared on the second floor.

"Let's let them sleep," whispered Delia as she tiptoed past the furry, feathered, and fuzzy-blanketed bodies snuggled on the floor. "We can get cleaned up for the County Fair later, once we're ready to go."

Willow sleepily fiddled with the splint that held her injured fingers. She was lying on her side, trying to get her feet onto the floor but failing. She looked like she could use a few more hours of sleep.

"How did you have time to make your bed, Delia?" she asked in a croaky voice.

Delia shrugged and put her finger to her lips to keep Willow from waking the rest of the room. The longer Sweet William, Bernice, and Gossie slept, the more time she and Willow would have for cooking.

"You two are awake early," whispered Uncle Liam as he shuffled past them in the hallway. "Going to the beach?" Then he added with a yawn, "I'm sorry you girls can't bake this trip—maybe you can cook together again at Christmastime."

Delia took Willow by the arm and set off down the staircase.

"Even your dad! Nobody thinks we can do anything this summer, Willow," she said, whispering into her cousin's curls. "Today is our chance to prove them wrong. Let's go!"

The morning was cloudless through the kitchen windows, and the rains of the past few days seemed finally to have passed. Delia was happy to find their cupcakes standing at attention on the table and ready for the final touches. Behind them stretched blue water and blue sky as far west as Delia could see.

"There's no better way to start the day than like this," Willow said, pouring two bowls of cereal and heading out to the back porch. "Come on!"

Delia followed her cousin outside and plopped down

on the top step beside her. They sat quietly crunching their breakfasts as the waves lapped on the shore down below. But then, right between bites of cereal, Delia heard something unusual in the yard.

It was high-pitched and twangy. And kind of awful. Delia couldn't help but tug at her ears. Willow's face puckered up like she'd tasted one of Mr. Henry's sour pickles.

"In the sky there is a rainbow . . ."

It was Violet and Darlene! They were practicing a song for the baby shower. And judging by the sound of it—*"raaaaaaiiiin-boooow"*—Delia figured they'd need a lot more practice if they were going to perform it tomorrow.

Thwack! Thwack! Thwack!

The screen door smacked as the uncles came out onto the porch. They dropped into chairs near Delia and Willow, looking curiously around the two yards.

"In the sky there is a raaaaaaiiiin-boooow . . ."

"Delvan," said Uncle Liam, pausing to take a sip of his coffee, "when did you and Deenie get cats?"

"I don't think that's cats," said Delia's dad. "I think it's Bernice howling at the moon. Or the sun. Or a satellite maybe?"

Uncle Jonathan rattled his head back and forth. "Whatever it is, it's pretty . . . *um* . . . impressive."

Before long, Grandma popped up from behind one of the azalea bushes and called to the uncles, putting them to work again on one of her gardening projects. They grudgingly said their good-byes. Then they set off to their shovels and mulch.

And the cousins set off for the kitchen again, this time to make chocolate-dipped bananas (with yellow sprinkles, of course), fruit tarts (with creamy yellow custard), and lemon bars.

"We've got lots to do," Delia announced. "Let's get cooking!"

It was a few hours later when Delia and Willow decided to take a break from all their dessert making. The kitchen was warm from the hot day and the even hotter oven.

"If good things happen in threes, today's the day for number one," Delia announced, tucking her knees inside her T-shirt. "I think we're going to win a blue ribbon at that County Fair this afternoon. Then tomorrow will be number two with the baby shower treats."

"And number three will be tomorrow night," Willow predicted. "I bet that's when Aunt Rosie has her baby!"

And as if to stir up more good luck, Willow tugged on her necklace, running the daisy pendant up and down its chain. Delia reached for the golden ring on her finger. She was eager to give it a few turns and be reminded of any good luck Grandma had passed along through the heirlooms.

But her finger felt bare.

She looked at both her hands. Nothing.

"My ring," she said in a sort of whisper-shout. "The one Grandma gave me! It's gone!"

"What do you mean?" Willow asked, her eyes scanning Delia's hands. "Did you lose it upstairs in your bed? Or the other night in the tent?"

Delia thought hard, trying to remember when she had it last. But her mind was a smoothie, her thoughts blending all together.

"I know I had it yesterday, when we were talking to our moms and Aunt Rosie," she said, her heart pounding.

Willow told her not to worry, her ring was bound to turn up someplace.

"That's what I'm afraid of," Delia said, grabbing hold of Willow's good hand. "I think I lost it when we were cooking! It could be in any of our desserts— the lemon cake, the lemon bars, the cookies, or the fruit tarts. Even the gingerbread. Willow, that ring could be in one of the cupcakes!"

Chapter 13
the ticking cupcake clock

It was noon when the cousins realized they had to stop.

They'd torn apart the lemon cake until it was nothing but yellow mush. They'd broken most of the yellow cookies and destroyed nearly half of the lemon bars. Now crumbs covered every inch of the kitchen's counter space and even parts of the floor. Bernice was helpful in cleaning up much of what Delia and Willow spilled. But still, the room was a mess.

And the ring was still missing.

"If we want to get those cupcakes to the contest by one o'clock, we've got to get ready," Willow said.

"What should we do?"

"Maybe I did lose it in the tent," Delia sighed, though she couldn't help eyeing the ice-cream cone cupcakes with suspicion. "I'd really hate to tear apart everything we made. What would be left to enter in the County Fair contest?"

Willow assured her that the ring would turn up. "Sweet William will find it near the broccoli bush," she offered hopefully. "Or in the crate next to Gossie's eggs. So don't worry about it anymore."

Delia said she'd try not to. Now it was time to

think about getting to the County Fair. All they needed was something to carry the cupcakes in—a couple of shoe boxes cut with holes to keep the cones from tipping over.

"I think I have two in my bedroom closet," she said. "We can change clothes while we're there. But we have to hurry!"

They were down the porch steps and across the yard in seconds, racing through the yellow house in search of the shoe boxes. And that's when they ran into Violet and Darlene on the staircase.

"We haven't talked to Uncle Jonathan yet about the baby shower," Darlene began, sitting down on the steps as if she wanted to have a long talk.

"Do you think we should play for him this afternoon?" wondered Violet, taking a seat beside Darlene and blocking the way. "Or at dinner? You know, let him hear the song we picked and how good we are."

"NO!" shouted Delia and Willow impatiently.

"I mean," sputtered Willow, "he heard you playing."

"And he said it was *pretty impressive*," added Delia

with a nervous tug on her braid. They didn't have time for this! They needed to get past their sisters and deliver those cupcakes to the fair, before it was too late.

"I think he had a few suggestions," Willow added quickly, edging around their sisters and up the next few steps. "Mostly it was just to keep on practicing!"

And Delia gave their sisters a big thumbs-up sign as she and Willow bounded up the rest of the staircase for those shoe boxes.

It was only moments later when they were back in the kitchen at Whispering Pines, the cupcakes packed and ready to go and the cousins wearing fresh T-shirts.

But how would they actually get their entry to the fair?

"We could ride bikes," suggested Delia, "but if we hit a bump, the cupcakes would get mashed."

"And it's too far to walk," Willow said. "I saw the Ferris wheel on the drive here. It must be a few miles away from us."

They had to ask someone to drive them there. And fast!

But their moms were already out with Aunt Rosie. Grandma was busy in the garden working the uncles to death. Their sisters and Sweet William couldn't help. And Cat and Mr. Henry were preoccupied with their pickling.

That left only one person: Grandpa.

They turned to the corner of the kitchen.

"Can you get us there?" Willow asked. She had begun shifting nervously from one flip-flop to the next as the deadline drew closer. "We're in a big hurry!"

Grandpa folded his newspaper and got to his feet, jangling his car keys in his hand. "I thought you'd never ask," he said, striding across the kitchen and into the yard toward the driveway. "Climb aboard the cupcake express!"

But it was more like the cupcake *depress*.

Delia and Willow had hopped into the backseat and slammed the doors, ready to go. But no matter how many times Grandpa turned the key, the engine sounded miserable.

"Again, Grandpa, please!" begged Delia, the cupcake shoe box balanced on her lap. "We've got to get this car to start."

Willow sat beside her, splotchy pink marks breaking out on her neck and cheeks.

"Where's your magic whisk, Delia?" she whispered, balancing the other shoe box. "We need you to turn this pumpkin into a carriage!"

To make matters worse, suddenly a long red fire truck pulled into the driveway behind them. Gravel crunched under its big wheels as it rolled to a stop and parked directly behind Grandpa's car. They were trapped.

Willow, Delia, and Grandpa pushed open their doors and jumped out.

"Is there another fire in the Arts and Eats cafe kitchen?" asked Grandpa.

"Is the yellow house all right?" exclaimed Delia.

"We're just making a follow-up visit," explained

the fire captain calmly. And he greeted Sweet William as he came running over. "We wanted to be sure you folks were all doing okay. And, to be honest, we were hoping to get a cookie."

Delia's heart was pounding. And Willow was bouncing nervously, springing up and down like a pogo stick. Delia peeked over at her cousin's cupcakes, making sure they were still upright.

Then she got a great idea.

"What about a trade?" she asked quickly. "If we give you a few cupcakes, would you be able to get us

to the County Fair? There's an important contest we need to get to, and it's minutes away!"

The captain took a bite and nodded, saying something that Delia thought sounded like *"Delicious!"* He told the cousins to climb aboard, along with Grandpa and Sweet William, too. And in no time, the bright red fire truck was speeding down the road toward the Saugatuck County Fair, lights flashing and sirens blaring.

Ice-Cream Cone Cupcakes with Sprinkles and a Cherry on Top

Ingredients:

½ cup (1 stick) butter, softened

1½ cups sugar

2 eggs

2 cups flour

½ teaspoon salt

1½ teaspoons baking powder

1 cup milk

2 teaspoons vanilla

24 flat-bottom ice-cream-cones

Directions:

1. Make sure you have an adult's help.

2. Heat the oven to 350 degrees.

3. Using an electric mixer, beat the butter and sugar together until light and fluffy.

4. Add in eggs and beat some more. Then pour in the flour, salt, baking powder, milk, and vanilla. Beat together for about 2 minutes, until everything is blended. Make sure you don't spatter batter all over your kitchen.

5. Stand up the cones in the muffin tins. Then spoon batter into each cone, filling only halfway up. If you fill too high, the cake will overflow.

6. Bake for about 25 minutes. Check doneness by sticking a tooth-pick into the cake. When it comes out clean, the cake is fully cooked.

7. While the cupcake cones cool, prepare the icing.

Icing ingredients:

½ cup (1 stick) butter, softened
3 cups powdered sugar, sifted
2 teaspoons vanilla

Pinch of salt

Directions:

1. Using an electric mixer, beat the butter until smooth.

2. Add in the powdered sugar, vanilla, and salt. Beat until combined, then raise the mixer speed and beat on high until icing is smooth and fluffy.

3. Once the cupcake cones are completely cooled, layer the icing on top to look like ice cream.

4. Gently drop rainbow sprinkles over icing. Then add a fresh cherry on top.

Makes about 24 cupcake cones.

Chapter 14
family is never embarrassing

W hy didn't you tell anyone you entered the cup- cake contest?" asked Grandpa. He was still shouting, even though they had already jumped off the truck and turned in their cupcakes. His ears hadn't quite adjusted to the lower volume. "I'm sure the whole family would love to come out here and support you girls!"

That was just the problem, Delia began. Willow was beside her, tugging at the bandage around her fingers. "Sometimes our family can be a little . . ."

"Loud?" said Sweet William.

"Colorful?" offered Grandpa, trying to be polite.

"Embarrassing," Delia and Willow said together.

Grandpa asked if they were any more embarrassing than a wailing, flashing fire truck.

"Our family can't top that," said Willow. "Can they?"

It only took a few minutes for them to find out.

They were standing inside the bright red barn that housed all the booths for the day's contests. They were just admiring the other cakes and cupcakes when Delia became distracted by three curious-looking hats.

And even more curious were the three heads beneath them.

"Mom? What are you guys doing here?" she asked, her voice higher than she meant it to be. "I thought you were out shopping for baby booties!"

"And what are you guys wearing on your heads?" squeaked Willow.

Delia's mom adjusted her big blue cowboy hat, while Aunt Rosie flicked one of the round tassels that hung from her wide-brimmed sombrero. Aunt Aggie ran her fingers through the long white feather on her hat, looking a lot like a pirate.

Delia and Willow cringed.

"We were just having a little fun," Delia's mom explained with a grin. And Delia spotted chocolate at the corner of her mom's mouth. "The County Fair was one of our favorite things to do as girls. So we came today as a last hurrah before Rosie has her baby."

Grandpa said he remembered when they were

too little to ride the Ferris wheel. And as the grown-ups swapped old memories, Willow nudged Delia's ribs with her elbow. She pointed at Aunt Rosie, who was taking a seat on a nearby bench and sneaking the last bites of a corn dog.

"They've probably eaten their way through the whole County Fair," whispered Willow, her voice low in Delia's ear. "They don't want us to know, since they would never let us have that much junk food!"

Delia looked thoughtfully from Aunt Rosie to their cupcakes. Everybody had summer secrets, though some were more secret than others.

Suddenly more bodies were swarming around Willow and Delia.

"So this is where you guys rushed off!"

It was their big sisters.

"Wh-what are you doing here?" stammered Willow.

"My wrists hurt from playing the ukulele so much," Violet began. "And Darlene needs ice cream to cool her throat after all that singing. So Grandma decided to bring us here."

And Delia saw a green gardening glove rise into the air behind them, fingers wiggling. "Hello, dears!"

Delia began trying to turn the family around, away from the cakes and cupcakes and toward the rides. Willow asked about the Ferris wheel and buying tickets.

But Darlene interrupted, saying she wanted an ice-cream cone just like the ones behind them in the contest. "Only it's so hot today, why aren't those ice creams melting?"

"That's what I wanted to know too," said Aunt Rosie from her bench. She was looking hungry as she rubbed her watermelon stomach. Delia noticed Willow take a quick step backward, so she wasn't too close to their aunt's beach-ball belly. "They look so delicious, I want to have them all!"

Delia was so proud of their cupcakes, she couldn't stop herself from describing the yellow cake inside the cones. And Willow explained how they were topped with frosting, not real ice cream.

But Violet and Darlene couldn't believe it. So they waved off their little sisters as if they didn't know what they were talking about.

"We know," Willow finally hollered, "because we made them!"

"*Ugh*," Delia moaned, slapping a hand to her forehead. "Looks like our cupcake secret isn't so secret anymore."

There were murmurs of surprise amid *oooooh*s and *aaaaah*s. But Delia's mom exclaimed the loudest. "With your injured fingers? How did you do it, Willow?" And she gently examined Willow's bruised fingers as if they were in the clinic at the hospital. "Maybe we underestimated you girls."

Willow gazed over at their platter of cupcakes and bounced in her flip-flops, her hair like coiled springs. Delia could see how proud she was.

"It's all right," Willow said. And, looping her arm through Delia's, she was beaming. "Everybody else might have doubted me, but Delia never did."

Just then three more faces appeared, sipping tall

cups of lemonade through curlicue straws. It was the three uncles, wearing dark sunglasses and sun hats, and looking almost as ridiculous as the three aunts. They acted as if they were trying not to be recognized. And when they caught sight of Grandma, Delia realized that's exactly who they were hiding from.

"Delvan, Liam, Jonathan!" called Grandma. "You three fellows . . ." And she stepped over, jabbing a green finger at their chests. The uncles looked as if they were caught. "You've worked so hard in the garden. Everybody deserves a break. I hope you're cooling off and having fun!"

Delia's dad let out a deep sigh of relief. And Uncle Liam clapped Uncle Jonathan on the back. They told everyone they'd already taken a ride on a waterslide, and now they were headed for the Ferris wheel.

"Wonderful," Grandma said. "But when we get home, I have a few marigolds that need planting."

The uncles' smiles dropped as fast as a plunging roller coaster.

"Let's hear it for Willow and Delia," cheered

Grandpa, turning everyone's attention back to the County Fair contest. "Their cupcakes are out of this world!"

And the whole family began clapping and shouting and making such a racket, people passing by the contest booths began to stare. Aunt Aggie and Aunt Rosie gave friendly waves, the feather and tassels on their hats bobbing happily. Sweet William was wailing like a fire truck's siren. The uncles were clapping

in rhythm now, creating a chant that sounded a lot like a war cry. Even Violet and Darlene were in on the frenzy, fingers in their mouths and whistling loudly.

"Our family isn't embarrassing at all," Willow said, tugging on the collar of her T-shirt and trying to disappear like a blushing turtle.

"Nope, not a bit," mumbled Delia. And she slipped her dad's sunglasses onto her nose and planted her mom's colorful cowboy hat on her head. "I wish we were back on that fire truck!"

Chapter 15
"we do!"

delia and Willow tried again to point the whole merry band of aunts and uncles and grandparents and cousins outside and toward the merry-go-round—or anywhere else that was far away from the cupcake contest.

But then Delia heard another voice cut through her family's cheering.

"What are y'all talking about?"

It was Cat. She was standing by the judges, and she didn't sound happy. Willow clutched Delia's arm as they slowly edged closer. Delia wanted to squeeze her eyes shut, knowing what Cat's face looked like

like when she was irritated.

"We forgot to tell her we were entering the contest," she whispered.

"How did she find out?" wondered Willow.

"I think those judges just told her!" Delia squeaked.

Cat and Mr. Henry were explaining to the judges about their pickling project. They were talking vinegar and dill and special spices, and what jars had the best lids. But the judges weren't interested in pickles. They wanted to talk cupcakes.

"As you can see," said one of the judges, pointing to the contest entry card, "there were two names written down, but then they were scratched out. And what is written in their place is plain to see."

Cat and Mr. Henry bent low to read the square white form.

"The Arts and Eats Café!" Cat hollered. And turning to Mr. Henry, she asked, "Now who on earth goes around entering contests and trying to cook for us?"

Delia nudged Willow with her shoulder, urging her to speak up.

Willow nudged her right back.

Finally, they both raised their hands.

"We do!"

Cat, Mr. Henry, and the whole big Bumpus family backed quickly away from the cupcake booth. Cat's expression was stony, and Mr. Henry took off his hat and put it right back on again at least four times. Delia and Willow pressed in close so Cat could hear them.

"We're so sorry!"

"We were going to tell you!"

"It all happened so fast!"

"Those chocolate cupcakes looked delicious!"

That last one was from Sweet William. And Willow glared at him with such a look, he knew to be quiet.

The uncles were ushering the rest of the family to get in line for the merry-go-round, moms included. Aunt Rosie went along too, saying she would ride anything that didn't go up and down.

"It's all right, girls," Cat began, taking a fried drumstick that Mr. Henry had bought from a food stand. "I should have known those cupcakes belonged to y'all the second I laid eyes on them. They're as clever as can be."

Delia was a bit relieved to hear Cat's compliment. But she still wasn't sure what Cat was thinking.

"With that wounded wing of yours, Willow," Cat said, "how in the world could y'all do any cooking?"

Willow sputtered a few words here and there until finally Delia spoke up.

"She's still as amazing as ever," she said proudly. "Nothing slows Willow down. Especially in the kitchen."

Cat said she believed the cousins were promising chefs. But she still had a few questions for them.

"You made sure not to mix up the sugar and the

salt, right?" she asked. Willow and Delia nodded.

"And the eggs," Cat said, pointing at them with the drumstick. "You counted each and every egg, right?"

Delia and Willow promised.

"And the frosting. Did you measure that vanilla? Too much will ruin it."

The cousins crossed their hearts, vowing that they made the cupcakes the very best they could. Cat said that was all she could ask for, though her face was still tight.

"I like your thinking, y'all," Cat said, fixing them both with one of her fierce looks. Delia was so nervous, she was practically pulling her ponytail right off her head. "A blue-ribbon prize from the County Fair is one of the best ways to get folks into our café. So the more we can bring home, the better. And I know you girls have your hearts in the right place, so I can't be angry."

But Delia could see that Cat's eyes were lingering on Willow's bandaged fingers. Did Cat want them to on Willow's bandaged fingers. Did Cat want them to withdraw from the contest? Did Cat still have doubts about what she and Willow could do?

Delia turned to Willow and gave her good hand a squeeze. And when she looked into her cousin's amber eyes, Delia knew they were both thinking the very same thing: *Just wait until we win that blue ribbon.*

Chapter 16
and the blue ribbon goes to . . .

They walked around the fairgrounds getting their fill of funnel cakes and cotton candy, not to mention tall cups of lemonade with silly straws. The whole family—except Aunt Rosie, that is—took rides on the Ferris wheel and a pair of camels, the go-carts and the spinning teacups. Violet and Darlene won stuffed animals at the ringtoss, and Sweet William surprised everyone by knocking down a tower of bottles in a single throw. But what he won came as no surprise: a buggy-eyed goldfish in a plastic bag.

"Another pet," Aunt Aggie said with a shake of her head. "But at least it won't make too much of a mess in the house."

Before long, Grandpa announced it was four o'clock. "Time to head back over to the contest area and see who the judges picked!"

And the Bumpus brigade set off in that direction.

While the fairgrounds had seemed enormous a few hours ago, now it was just a matter of seconds before the bright red barn came into view. Delia began to jog in her flip-flops, urging Willow to hurry up.

"Okay, let's run!" she said as her heart beat faster in anticipation. And they took off down the twisting path, passing the smelly cows and even smellier pigs.

"Wait for us," called Cat. "I want to be the first to lay eyes on the blue ribbon!"

When they finally reached the judging area, Willow and Delia led the way past booth after booth of prize-winning quilts, lavender soaps, needlepoint projects, and giant pumpkins.

When they rounded the last corner, Delia froze in her tracks.

In the center of the table marked CAKES & CUP-CAKES was a blue ribbon the size of a cabbage, two shiny blue flaps stretching onto the white tablecloth. It was propped up next to a single cupcake on a plate.

Only that cupcake had brown chocolate frosting instead of vanilla. There were no rainbow sprinkles. No ice-cream cone to hold it up. No bright red cherry on top.

"We didn't win," sighed Delia. "They didn't like our cupcakes."

Cat waved her arms toward the other entries in the contest, complaining. There were platters of sliced cakes and half-eaten cupcakes everywhere, left behind by the hungry judges. But then she pointed at one plate that was separated, a sign taped to its rim.

"It's not that the judges didn't like your cupcakes, y'all," said Cat, pointing at the sign. "It's that your cupcakes were knocked out of the contest. Look!"

In bold black lettering was written a single word:

DISQUALIFIED

Chapter 17
bad-luck threes

What do you mean *disqualified*?" Cat was asking the judges for the fifth or sixth time. "Those desserts might not have looked like cupcakes, but that's no reason to keep these girls from competing!"

Two of the judges got to their feet, straightening their shoulders and looking serious.

"My name is Gloria Hightower," one explained, patting the enormous tower of hair that was piled atop her head. "I'm president of the local hospital, chairwoman of the County Fair advisory board, and a graduate of the Bon-Bon School of Pastry. I like to think that as a dessert judge, I'm a pretty sharp cookie—pun intended!" And she let out a hiccupping laugh.

"Well, your cookie just crumbled, if you ask me," Cat said hotly. She didn't crack a smile.

"It wasn't the use of non-cupcake material that disqualified your entry," Ms. Hightower began, nodding toward the ice cream cones. "It wasn't because the dessert didn't *look* like a cupcake. We actually applaud such creative thinking."

Cat was getting impatient. Her voice was sharp as she demanded to know the reason why.

"This entry was disqualified," Ms. Hightower continued, pausing to take a deep breath as she eyed Delia and Willow, "because one of the judges bit into a golden ring. It could have cracked his tooth!"

Cat gasped in surprise, and Willow put her hand on Delia's shoulder. But Delia could only drop her head. This was all her fault.

She'd lost the ring.

Lost the contest.

Lost the chance to help the café.

"And as you know if you read the County Fair handbook," Ms. Hightower was saying, "prizes are not allowed in any food entered into the contests. They pose a dangerous choking hazard to myself and the other judges!"

Delia couldn't speak. So Willow started explaining that they weren't including prizes in their cupcakes. It was just a mistake. But her voice was shaky, and finally she just asked if they could have the ring back.

"It means a lot to our family," Willow said. And

Delia felt her cousin's curls press in against her cheek.

If their grandmother was nearby to notice, she didn't say a word. Delia hoped her sagging shoulders made it clear to Grandma just how sorry she was.

Ms. Hightower introduced the judge standing beside her. She said his name was Chester Bacon. "He's the one who bit into your prize."

"It wasn't a prize," Willow said again, a little frustration in her voice. "It was a mistake."

Chester Bacon reached into his pocket as if to give them the ring, but his hand came out empty. "I seem to have misplaced it," he said, looking up and down the judging table. "Perhaps it went home with one of the other judges—they've already left for the day."

Delia clutched Willow's arm. The ring was gone? This cupcake contest kept getting worse by the minute! How could she tell their grandmother what she'd done?

The knot in Delia's stomach felt like it had moved to her heart. She could barely breathe.

"We have to get that ring back," Delia told the judge, leaning in close so he could hear her. She used her crossing-guard voice, speaking as slowly and calmly as she could. "Is there anything you can do? Can you call the other judges? Can you tell us where they are? Because it's really important we find it."

Mr. Bacon nodded like he understood. He told Delia he'd do his very best to locate her ring and return it.

"You can reach us at the Arts and Eats Café," Willow said, her arm on Delia's shoulder. "If you find the ring, please stop by."

As the whole Bumpus brigade left the judges and made its way to the parking lot, Willow tried to cheer Delia up.

"It may seem like we're in the middle of bad-luck threes," she was saying, "but we're not. We found your missing ring—sort of. At least we know it's not in Lake Michigan. Or in some stranger's tummy. And now we have a whole year to get ready for the next contest."

But Delia wasn't buying it.

"First I lost my ring in the cupcake batter, then I lost us the blue-ribbon prize," she told Willow, climbing into her dad's car and sliding into the seat behind her mom. She blinked hard to keep her eyes from tearing. "And now I've probably lost that ring forever," she whispered. "There's no getting around it, Willow. It *is* bad-luck threes!"

As the car pulled onto the road, Delia's mom turned in her seat toward Delia. "Losing Grandma's ring is a big deal," she began, her voice stern. "I think that's far more important than losing a cupcake contest. You're going to have to talk to Grandma."

Delia leaned her forehead against the window, wishing she could wave her magic whisk and start everything over again.

"Honestly, Delia," her mom continued, "you've

got to forget about that contest and *move on*."

But that was just the thing worrying Delia the most. If they didn't do something to bring more customers into the café, they all would have to *move on*. And that meant leaving the yellow house behind.

raindrops began to fall on the drive back home. And the sky matched Delia's mood: heavy, gray, stormy. Once they reached Whispering Pines, she and Willow went right to the kitchen.

Thwack! Thwack!

Bernice and Gossie issued nervous wags and honks from under the table, probably happy the family was back home but still not brave enough to come out during another thunderstorm. Sweet William came in next and slipped under the table to ride out the storm beside his two best friends.

"I'm going to introduce everybody to my new

goldfish," he announced from underneath the table. "I think I'll call him Bubbles."

It wasn't too much later when Grandpa came into the kitchen. He asked Delia and Willow to pull out the lemonade pitcher and two glasses.

"One for me," he said. And then the screen door squeaked as someone stepped in behind Grandpa.

"And one for me, y'all."

It was Cat. Delia looked at her with wide eyes, wishing the day had gone better. She tried to summon her calmest voice. But that worry knot had tied up her insides again.

It was Grandpa who spoke as the two cousins filled the glasses.

"I'm sorry the blue ribbon didn't go home with you girls today," he said, pausing for a sip. "And I'm sorry this year's vacation is getting rained out. But I can tell you what I'm *not* sorry for. And that is listening to your plans for Rosie's baby shower."

Delia shot a look at Willow, and then they both turned to Cat. Just as they'd kept the County Fair contest secret—for a while, at least—they hadn't told anyone about baking for Aunt Rosie's party, either. Most importantly, Cat. But still, Grandpa must have overheard them talking about lemon cookies and lemon cake. And what he hadn't heard or seen, he'd probably smelled.

"Girls, Cat and I were just talking on the ride home from the fairgrounds. And she told me she's about to head into the café kitchen for a long night of cooking for Aunt Rosie's party. If you two chefs have made anything for tomorrow's baby shower, I'm sure that would be a bright spot amid the gloom. Or as we say in the flower business, she'd be *glad*iolus."

Delia picked up the lemonade pitcher and filled her own glass. She gulped it down, feeling the tart juice clear her throat. They had planned to tell Cat about the yellow desserts. But with the messy search for Delia's ring, things had gotten a little complicated in the Whispering Pines kitchen.

She tried to remember what food was left.

"We have a few things to show you," she finally

said, setting down her glass and taking Cat by the arm. And she nodded at Willow to open the freezer. "Willow and I probably should have talked with you about this secret too."

"Maybe you'll forget all about today's contest when you see what we've made," Willow said, a little bounce in her step. Then she added, "I hope you both will."

As Willow set down the trays of frozen bananas, the container of fruit tarts, and what remained of the cookies and lemon bars, Delia felt a hint of a smile begin to take over her mouth. It was hard to be droopy when Willow was bouncy.

"Basically," Delia said, her eyes looking from Willow to Cat, "Aunt Rosie's shower comes down to just one word."

And the cousins summed it up at exactly the same time:

"Yellow!"

When Cat saw the lemon-colored treats laid out before her, Delia thought she was going to fall over. So she and Willow grabbed the nearest stool and helped her sit down.

Delia couldn't bring herself to mention the lemon cake they'd destroyed searching for the ring. Thank goodness they'd taken a moment to clean up.

"Willow Sweeney," Cat began, and she gently reached for Willow's bandaged hand, "how in the world were you able to do any mixing or baking or stirring? When I saw your fingers on Wednesday, I didn't think you could even hold a spoon. If I thought you could, I'd have asked you girls to be my helpers."

And with Cat's Mississippi twang, it came out sounding like *hayl-pers*.

"What? We didn't think you wanted us," Willow said, her eyes blinking back tears.

"Maybe you thought we were too young or not interested," Delia said. "Or you wanted our sisters instead of us."

"Or," Willow said softly, holding up her hand, "you just didn't think we could do it."

"I'm sorry for ever doubting y'all," Cat said. And spreading her arms wide, she added, "Just look at what you've done over here. This makes me as happy as a woodpecker in a lumberyard."

Cat pulled them close for a hug.

"I've been so focused on tomorrow's pickling contest, I'm not thinking straight. I haven't done nearly enough for Rosie's shower, not to mention the desserts to sell over at the café. Looking at these treats of yours, I might have to let y'all write the Arts and Eats menu."

With a few more hugs and squeezes, Cat thanked the cousins for their yellow surprises. Then she said her good-byes to Grandpa, Sweet William, and the growing zoo beneath the table and headed for the screen door.

"I'd better scoot my boots," she said. "Y'all have saved me time with those desserts. But I've still got to whip up the finger sandwiches and little quiches. Only no bacon this time—I learned my lesson at last year's wedding shower!"

Thwack!

Grandpa sat down at the table and gave them both a knowing wink. Whispering Pines was quiet now, the rest of the family probably having dinner next door at the café. He was eager to get back to their gingerbread beach houses.

"When we left off last night, I think you two girls were putting up a licorice porch railing," he said. "Sweet William and I were tackling the chocolate shingles. With so much rain this week, we all need a sturdy roof over our heads."

And as if to agree with Grandpa, lightning lit up the yard outside. A loud clap of thunder quickly followed. Bernice let out a whimper and dug her way farther under the table toward the wall. Gossie dove into her cardboard box with the eggs. Only Bubbles seemed unfazed as he swam in his bowl.

Delia and Willow stepped over to the far counter and gently lifted the tray holding the gingerbread project. They carried it to the table and placed it in the center, where Grandpa could reach it too. Then they plunked down the bowls of white icing and a few knives for spreading.

"Don't forget, we can use these for decorating," Willow said, reaching into her shorts pocket with her good hand and pulling out what was left of Grandpa's bag of gumdrops and jelly beans. "I think they're still soft enough."

After a few moments, Sweet William timidly climbed out from under the table and brushed at his knees. He snapped off two small pieces of extra gingerbread and slipped them down to Bernice and Gossie as a comforting snack. And sliding into a chair beside Grandpa, he examined the mound of brightly colored candies.

"I could make these gumdrops into kids or grown-ups—like the Clay Family and the Twig People," he said.

"You could call them the Gumdrop Gang," suggested Delia. She was happy to see her little cousin feeling braver about the storms. And she could tell Grandpa was happy too.

"Hey, Grandpa," Sweet William said, his eyes fixed on the dark clouds over the lake. "What kind of flowers do we need with all this rain?"

Grandpa, Delia, and Willow raised their eyebrows, surprised that Sweet William was able to tell a joke amid all his worrying. And when Grandpa answered that he didn't know, Sweet William turned to face them with a broad grin.

"Sunflowers, of course!"

Chocolate-Dipped Bananas on a Stick

Ingredients:

8 bananas
16 Popsicle sticks
24 ounces chocolate (the cousins prefer semisweet)
3 tablespoons butter
Assorted toppings (like chopped nuts, sprinkles, granola)

Directions:

1. Make sure you have an adult's help.

2. Measure up to the halfway point of each banana, and cut in half. Poke a Popsicle stick into the flat, cut side of each one. Lay the bananas in rows on a cookie sheet lined with wax paper or parchment paper.

3. Freeze the bananas for about 1 hour.

4. In a wide, low bowl, microwave the chocolate and butter for about 1 minute. Do not burn the chocolate! Gently stir it. If it is creamy, go to Step 5. If it is not, pop it back in the microwave for another minute or until it's fully melted.

5. Have a few plates ready for toppings. You can prepare sprinkles (either rainbow or solid colors), chopped peanuts, granola bits, even crushed candy like a toffee bar.

6. Dip the frozen banana pop in the chocolate. Then immediately hold it over one of the toppings plates. Shake or spoon the topping over the entire banana. Then lay the banana pop onto the lined cookie sheet.

7. Once all the bananas have been dipped and sprinkled in toppings and they are lined up on the cookie sheet, put them back into the freezer for another hour.

8. Use a thick block of Styrofoam to serve the banana pops. Poke the sticks into the block to stand them up straight. Watch out for hungry little brothers, and enjoy!

Chapter 19
a cupcake standoff

Willow and Delia woke up early Saturday morning, this time in Delia's bright green bedroom. The night had been noisy with the pounding rain, the rattling thunder, and the snoring guests. Bernice, Gossie, Sweet William, and now Bubbles had camped out with them again.

"You know, geese don't exactly snore," Delia pointed out, a yawn escaping as she spoke. "It's more like a low honk."

"Did you learn that at zoo camp?" Willow asked, groggily climbing out of her sleeping bag on Delia's floor.

"No," answered Delia, getting to her feet beside the cardboard box, "I learned it from sleeping next to Gossie all night!"

While the rest of their room continued in noisy slumber, the cousins slipped down the hall to the bathroom and got themselves ready for the baby shower. Willow put on one of Delia's sundresses, a green one with a single yellow flower embroidered in the front. Delia chose a pale blue one with white polka dots. They decided to fix each other's hair, though Delia could barely get a headband in place amid her cousin's thick curls. She decided to pin a yellow daisy just above one of Willow's ears instead.

Once they brushed their teeth and washed their faces—was it the first time so far this week? Delia wasn't sure—they carried their flip-flops and tiptoed down the stairs and across the squishy yard to the Whispering Pines kitchen.

And that's when they put on the most important thing for the whole day.

White aprons.

"Delia, could we make another batch of cupcakes? Maybe chocolate ones?" Willow asked. "After yesterday's contest, I want to make something really amazing. Just to remind ourselves that we can."

Delia shrugged. "We already lost the County Fair contest. Now nobody but our family will know how good our cupcakes are." And then, trying to swallow the lump that caught in her throat, she added, "It won't help with business at the Arts and Eats Café."

"But remember," Willow pointed out, "we didn't

lose that contest because our cupcakes were bad. We were disqualified. There's a big difference!"

Delia just couldn't get excited about any more baking.

"It's bad-luck threes," she told Willow. "What's the point when we already know it will end in disaster?"

Willow looked out the window. "Where are those hummingbirds?" she asked. "Because we could use a little good luck now—and fast!"

Delia let out a heavy sigh. Her heart wasn't in it this morning, not when she'd messed up so badly yesterday. Winning a blue ribbon was the most important thing she could have done for her family. Just thinking about it made her want to climb back into her sleeping bag.

And how could she ever face Grandma to tell her she'd lost the ring?

Delia untied the bow on her apron and took it off, folding it into a neat rectangle.

"There were just two things we set out to do this

week, Willow: bake for the baby shower and for the contest," she began. "We've already made enough desserts for one. And I lost us the other. So why do anything else?"

"You can't quit now, Delia," Willow said, her voice pleading. "Just because the County Fair contest didn't go our way doesn't mean everything is hopeless."

"Yes, it kind of does," argued Delia. "I wanted to make things better for the café. But I didn't. In fact, I made everything worse when I lost Grandma's ring. So what's the point of wasting the morning in here? I should go walk on the beach or fill the hummingbird feeders."

Willow set the cocoa down with a thud. A small puff of brown powder shot into the air. Delia hadn't seen Willow angry like this before.

"*Wasting the morning*? You think making more cupcakes will be wasting your morning? Fine," Willow said, picking up an egg with her left hand and cracking it angrily on the rim of the mixing bowl. "You can be that way."

And she began stirring with what Delia thought was a bit too much energy.

"Nobody thought we could do anything this week," Willow continued, her voice sounding a little huffy. Her splint made a clicking noise against the bowl. "And look at all the things we did."

Delia corrected her. "Nobody thought *you* could do anything, Willow. But you did. And you were as great as ever. On the other hand, everybody thought I was all right. But I failed. At everything."

Just thinking about her ring—Grandma's ring—in the cupcake batter made Delia wince. What if she'd made that County Fair judge sick? What if she never saw their family heirloom again?

Willow set the bowl down, putting her hands on her hips with an angry growl. "A real fairy godmother wouldn't quit just because something didn't work out," she told Delia. "A real fairy godmother would know that you have to try again. And again. *And again.*

"And a real chef would too," Willow continued. "Because the first thing I ever learned about cooking works for just about everything else: You never know how something will turn out until you give it a try."

Delia walked away, over toward the big window and the lake. She turned her back to her cousin, though she peeked over her shoulder once or twice.

Willow picked up the mixing bowl and headed over to the opposite counter, so that her back was to Delia.

And there they stood for a good long while. One cousin was busy brooding; the other was busy stirring.

It was a cupcake standoff.

Before long, Willow's dad shuffled in and fixed a pot of coffee. He must have sensed the tension in the air, because he quickly turned around and shuffled right back out.

The only sound in the kitchen was the *drip, drip, drip* of the coffeemaker. After a few minutes, once the machine went silent, Delia could hear her cousin pour the coffee into a mug. She again peeked over her shoulder at Willow, though neither chef was speaking. But when she saw Willow dump a whole mug of the black and bitter brew into the mixing bowl, Delia gasped.

"What are you thinking, Willow? You'll ruin the batter!"

But Willow just looked up and grinned.

"Finally, you're talking to me again," she sighed. "Aunt Rosie isn't allowed to drink coffee while she's expecting a baby. So I thought that if we added just a little coffee to flavor the cupcakes, she could get a taste of it without having too much."

"Is that in the recipe?" Delia wanted to know. "Or

are you just winging it, like last summer?"

Willow smiled.

"Like I said: You never know how something will turn out until you give it a try." And she handed the chocolatey whisk to Delia. "It's the same with the desserts we're making for the baby shower. We'll never know if something good will come of them until we make them and serve them at the party."

Delia took the drippy whisk in her hand, fighting the smile that was taking over her mouth. She thought about Willow. Her cousin had a way of always finding the bright side of things. And that meant Delia would find it too, in her own way.

"A little while ago, you called this whisk my fairy-godmother wand," she told Willow. "Well, I think I'm ready to wave it."

Chocolate Surprise Cupcakes with Sunshine Frosting

Ingredients:
- ½ cup (1 stick) butter, softened
- 2 cups sugar
- 2 eggs
- ½ cup plain yogurt
- 1 teaspoon vanilla
- 1¾ cups flour
- ¾ cup cocoa (unsweetened)
- 2 teaspoons baking powder
- 1 cup brewed coffee, room temperature

Directions:

1. Make sure you have an adult's help.

2. Heat the oven to 350 degrees.

3. Line cupcake tin with paper liners.

4. Using an electric mixer, cream the butter and sugar for about 2 minutes.

5. Add in the eggs, yogurt, and vanilla, and beat well for a minute more.

6. In a second bowl, mix the dry ingredients.

7. Pour the dry ingredients into the wet mixture, and beat together.

8. Add in the coffee.

9. Scoop the batter into the cupcake tin, and bake for about 20 minutes. You'll know it's done when a toothpick poked into the center of a cupcake comes out clean.

Let them cool completely.

Sunshine yellow frosting:

Ingredients:
½ cup (1 stick) butter, softened

8 ounces (1 package) cream cheese, softened

1 teaspoon vanilla

2 cups powdered sugar

Yellow food coloring

Directions:

1. Using an electric mixer, beat the butter and cream cheese together for about 3 minutes, until smooth and creamy.

2. Add in the vanilla and mix some more. Slowly pour in the powdered sugar and beat together.

3. Pour in a few drops of yellow food coloring, and mix completely.

4. Stop the machine and use a fresh spoon to sample the icing. If it is thick enough and tastes perfect, move to Step 5. If not, add a ¼ cup more sugar and turn on the mixer again. Don't take another sample until you've turned the machine off!

5. Once the cupcakes are cooled, spread the sunshine frosting on the tops and share.

Makes about 18 cupcakes.

Chapter 20
agapanthus, gardenia, and rose

delia and Willow had just finished spreading the cupcakes with a bright yellow frosting when Delia's mom stepped into the kitchen. She was tugging on a roll of white medical tape, telling Willow to stand still while she taped up her fingers.

"It's okay, Aunt Deenie," Willow began. "My hand feels just fine."

"You can never be too careful," Delia's mom was saying as she wrapped and pressed and gently pulled. Willow gave Delia a desperate look, but Delia just shrugged. There was no stopping her mom when she got into hospital mode.

Thankfully, Aunt Aggie marched in next with her pencils and her party checklist.

"Tablecloths? Check!"

"Candles? Check!"

"Vases? Check!"

Last night's storms had finally passed, and their moms said the day was expected to be sunny and free of rain—at least for most of the afternoon.

Grandma pushed through the dining room door moments later and poured herself a cup of coffee. Its warm, nutty aroma drew Uncle Liam back in— though this time he was out of his pajamas and dressed for the day. Uncle Jonathan and Grandpa were right behind him.

It was only a matter of minutes before the whole house began humming with activity, as everyone pitched in to get the grounds set up for the baby shower.

"But first, before we get too far with Rosie's special day," began Grandma, waving her green-gloved hands over her head to get everyone's attention.

"There's something special in the yard, and I'd like to show Grandpa what it is. I chased him off a few days ago, so that Liam, Delvan, and Jonathan could help me get it ready."

And as she led Grandpa outside and into the connected yards, Darlene and Violet and the others arrived from the yellow house.

"Surprise!" Grandma cheered. "I've shared some of the Bumpus family heirlooms with the grandkids. And now I want to share this one, here in Saugatuck, with Grandpa. These come from our old flower shop in Chicago. It's what I've been up to each day, croaking orders like a toad." And turning to Grandpa, she said, "I hope you'll forgive me."

"It makes me think of a toad's favorite flower," Grandpa said, slipping an arm around Grandma's shoulder and giving it a squeeze. "The crocus."

Grandma playfully jabbed his side and told him to take a look. And what he saw, and Delia and the whole family too, was beautiful. It made Grandpa pull a hankie from his pocket and blow his nose.

Grandma had planted flowers and shrubs around an ancient-looking stone birdbath. It was standing alongside the new stone walkway that connected Whispering Pines to Delia's yellow house. There was even an iron bench beside it, which had the name of their flower shop written in a black scroll at the top: *Bumpus Blooms.* Grandma said it was perfect for her and Grandpa to sit down and look back across the water toward Chicago.

"Are those agapanthus flowers?" asked Willow, pointing at the tall purple blooms beside the birdbath.

"They certainly are," Grandma said, "and next to them are gardenias and, as you can probably guess, a rosebush."

Delia saw her mom dabbing her eyes now. Aggie, Deenie, and Rosie, that's what everybody called the three Bumpus sisters. But their real names were Agapanthus, Gardenia, and Rose, in honor of Grandpa's three favorite flowers.

Just then a truck pulled into the gravel driveway, and Mr. Henry marched off for the front of the house to speak with the driver. And in minutes, round tables and white chairs were unloaded onto the lawn. Delia watched the uncles arrange them across the yard.

Darlene and Violet got to work unfurling yellow tablecloths. Grandma filled low vases with fragrant flowers like yellow freesia and white sweet pea. Aunt Aggie and Delia's mom set out round candles on every table. Sweet William, wearing his blue swim goggles, flippers, and snorkel, joined Grandpa in setting up a square table near the big tree on the side of Whispering Pines. Grandpa said guests could stack their baby gifts there.

"Why are you wearing swim trunks?" asked Violet as she hurried past them. "You should get dressed already. You might not have time to change later."

Sweet William glanced down at his striped trunks and back up again.

"I am dressed," he said, sounding confused. He was pushing Gossie's cardboard box to a shady spot beside the table. "I'm sure not walking around here naked. So what else are we supposed to wear to a shower?"

Violet rolled her eyes but was too busy to point him back upstairs. And Grandpa just grinned and said Sweet William had made the perfect choice for a shower.

Once the last long table was in place—pushed beside the length of the porch and covered in a checkered yellow tablecloth—it was time to bring out the food. Cat carried trays of her sandwiches. She had made tiny cucumber and cream cheese squares, little turkey and green apple rectangles, and thick egg salad circles.

But it was Delia and Willow's desserts that got the most cheers. Delia set the pretty white cake plate in the center of the table. It was piled high with lemon bars, each one dusted with snowy powdered sugar. Willow was next, toting a special three-tiered stand with her good hand. It was stacked with miniature fruit tarts that Delia thought looked like tiny cups of rainbows—the round red cherries, bright blueberries, sunny orange peaches, and green grapes decorating each one.

"May I have one of these banana pops?" asked Sweet William as Willow and Delia delivered the next two platters onto the table. The chocolate-dipped bananas covered in yellow sprinkles were hard to resist. But Delia chased Sweet William off, saying nobody was allowed to sneak anything until the party started.

"What about cupcakes?" asked Mr. Henry, taking off his sun hat and fanning himself. "Will you serve any today? Whether the judges at the Saugatuck County Fair know it or not, girls, your cupcakes are a highlight of the summer."

Delia touched her bare finger, wishing the ring were there.

"Hold on to your sun hats," Willow told them. "We'll be right back with a cupcake surprise."

Once they were back inside the kitchen, Delia and Willow finished arranging the bright yellow treats on each level of the tallest display stand. It was four tiers high, just like last summer's wedding cake. Cat had given it to them at Christmas—her way of saying thank you for saving the wedding reception.

"Last summer we were celebrating Aunt Rosie's wedding," began Delia. "And today we're celebrating Rosie's baby. I can't wait to meet our new cousin. She should be here any day now."

Willow was on her tiptoes, reaching for the top tier of the cupcake stand. Her expression was more serious than ever. "Even though I don't like baby talk," she said, moving a few more cupcakes into place, "I do want this baby shower to go well. Because making the desserts, well, this is how we prove it to everyone."

Delia raised her eyebrow. "Prove what?"

"That we're really good at this," Willow said. "That last summer wasn't a fluke. That we're, well . . . chefs."

Delia watched the way her cousin was biting her lip. This shower meant so much to Willow. Thank goodness the family ring wasn't in one of these desserts. If she ruined the baby shower for Willow, Delia would feel a hundred times more awful than she already did.

"But I'm a little afraid that we might be stuck in bad-luck threes after all," Willow began. "What if it turns out to be another disaster like yesterday? Only it's my fault?"

Delia shook her head. They'd worked as hard as they could to get these desserts right. "Good luck or bad luck, who knows? We can't be afraid to try. So let's go."

Just as they did last summer—only Willow was using one hand instead of two—the cousins gently lifted their delicious handiwork off the center island in the Whispering Pines kitchen, across the wooden porch, and down the stairs into the yard.

"*Ta-da!*" they announced as they set the giant cupcake tower onto the yellow table. Aunt Rosie was in the yard now, and she joined the rest of the family in *ooooohing* and *aaaaahing* over the four-story dessert tower.

"Everything's gorgeous!" said Delia's mom. "I can't believe you girls!" And holding up Willow's injured hand, she studied her fingers and the new white tape in disbelief. "Yesterday it was cupcake cones, and now this? What a recovery!"

"So many yellow desserts," Aunt Rosie whispered, looking a little stunned. "I'm sorry we ever doubted you."

"I imagine it tastes as good as it looks too," said Aunt Aggie with a grin.

Willow leaned toward Delia and whispered, "Let's hope so!"

After a few more minutes of the aunts' fussing, Mr. Henry cleared his throat and took off his sun hat to make a sort of speech.

"I apologize," he said with a bow, "but it seems the County Fair contest for best pickling takes place now. And if Ms. Catherine and I are to enter our jars on time, we must leave you. It is unfortunate. But also, it is hard to resist the call of the pickle."

Cat said she'd hired a few extra hands to work over at the café during Rosie's shower. So nobody was to worry about Arts & Eats for a few hours.

"All that's left for y'all to do is welcome the guests and enjoy your shower!"

Chapter 21
bacon and cupcakes

After an hour (or maybe even two) of arranging and organizing and rearranging, the yard was declared officially ready and the first guests arrived. There were Uncle Jonathan's parents and brothers to greet, along with their wives and kids and friends, too. Delia recognized most of the guests as they filed into the yard, but there were some she had never seen before.

"Who do you think they are?" whispered Willow.

She was pointing across the lawn at the back porch of the café. Two unfamiliar guests were walking purposefully down Grandma's new stone path toward the baby shower. "Party crashers? Maybe they're looking for free food?"

"Maybe not," Delia said softly. "My mom is saying hello to that lady like she knows her. I think they work together at the hospital. Her face and that hair look a little familiar."

Suddenly, Willow began to bounce in her flip-flops.

"Of course you recognize her," she said, her curls boinging on her shoulders. "That's the judge from the County Fair yesterday. I bet she's here with that other judge to tell us we've won the cupcake contest after all!"

They hurried over to Delia's parents to hear what was going on. Delia's mom was introducing the tall lady with the even taller hair—Ms. Hightower was her name—to Delia's dad.

"I am so glad we had a reason to come here today," Ms. Hightower was saying. "We just took a tour of your splendid café and art gallery, Mr. Dees. It's very impressive. You're a talented artist. And the hospital committee has been looking for a local painter recently. You see, we've just built a new wing at the hospital, and we need to hang art on all those blank walls. Perhaps you . . ."

Delia's head began to spin. Was the hospital lady really interested in her dad's paintings? She could hardly believe her ears!

Delia wanted to stay and hear more, but she couldn't. That's because Willow had grabbed her by the arm and was dragging her over to Aunt Aggie and Uncle Liam. Bernice was pressed in close as they talked with the other County Fair judge—the one with the funny name.

Delia knew it had something to do with Sunday mornings.

Was he Mr. Waffles?

Mr. Syrup?

"Mr. Bacon!" she shouted, happy that her memory had come through. And whispering to Willow, she added, "Maybe that's why Bernice is staying so close."

Willow covered her mouth with her bandaged fingers, trying to hide a chuckle.

"That's right, ladies," he said, extending his hand for Delia, then a bit awkwardly for Willow, to shake. "I'm Chester Bacon. I was just talking with these folks about yesterday's cupcake contest."

Delia let out a nervous hiccup, which made Willow jab her with an elbow.

"There's a reason Ms. Hightower and I stopped by today," he was saying. And he reached his hand into his pants pocket. Only this time, when he pulled it out, the golden ring was there. He passed it to Delia.

"The good news is that I was able to track down your missing jewelry."

Delia heaved a sigh as she clutched the ring. Not only was she relieved to feel it in her hands again, but she also couldn't help but cling to a teeny-tiny hope that they'd won the County Fair contest.

"And the bad news?" asked Willow.

"The bad news is that—as much as Ms. Hightower and I enjoyed your cupcakes—once a blue ribbon is awarded, it cannot be taken back."

Delia slipped the ring on her finger, the news stinging her ears. She was grateful to have Grandma's family heirloom back, no doubt about it. But still, it was hard to shake her feelings about losing the County Fair contest.

If only her plan to get more customers for the Arts & Eats Café had worked.

At least the other judge was interested in her dad's paintings, so that was more good news. She tried to focus on that, but Mr. Bacon was still speaking.

He was saying a few nice things about Arts & Eats and strong coffee. But what he said next made Delia perk up her ears and really pay attention. Mr. Bacon told them he not only liked what he saw at the café, but what he tasted, too.

That gave Delia an idea.

"Keep talking with him," she whispered urgently into Willow's ear. "I'll be right back!"

Then she hurried off toward the food table.

Willow was left stuttering with Mr. Bacon and her parents. Delia could hear her ask Mr. Bacon about the County Fair cupcake judging.

"What did you and the other judges like about the winner's cupcakes?" Willow was saying. "Were they moist? Crumbly?"

When Delia returned moments later, Mr. Bacon

was describing the tastiness of the winning cupcake's frosting. Delia was carrying a full plate of desserts—a lemon bar, a chocolate-covered banana on a stick, two of their coffee-chocolate cupcakes with yellow frosting, and one of the prettiest fruit tarts ever made. Or at least Delia thought it was.

"For me?" asked Mr. Bacon. And with a chuckle, he said, "Don't mind if I do."

Delia explained how these desserts *might* be on the Arts & Eats menu soon.

"The café has only been open for a few months, so Cat Sutherland is still working out the details," Willow added, her breathing a little fast.

"We're Cat's . . . sous-chefs," Delia said, trying hard to remember how to pronounce that word. "We help her out with the, *ah*, sweets."

The cousins stood there watching every movement of Chester Bacon's jaw as he chewed. Even though someone else went home with the blue ribbon, Delia wanted these judges to know what a winning dessert really tasted like.

Uncle Liam began talking newspapers and about his job at the *Chicago Tribune*, where he was a food critic. Mr. Bacon nodded, his cheeks too full to speak, but his eyes were on his plate.

Finally, he took a breath.

"I'm not sure how they do things over in Chicago. It's a big city, and the *Tribune* is a big newspaper. But over on this side of Lake Michigan, we do things my way." And here he paused, setting his plate down and hitching his pants up. "I'm the editor of the *Saugatuck Times*. And I'm also the sports reporter, advice columnist for the heartbroken, cartoonist, and sometimes I even deliver newspapers onto front porches. But the part of my job I love best is writing about food.

"What I can tell you is this," he said, squaring himself to face Delia and Willow directly. "I'm going to write a review of the Arts and Eats Café. And I'm going to run it on the front page of my newspaper with a big photo of these cupcakes. Saugatuck readers need to know about this café's delicious food!"

Delia and Willow couldn't believe their ears. They

began to hug and laugh and whoop and holler for joy. And they were just about to tumble onto the lawn in their usual way when something stopped them.

It was the strumming of a ukulele, a little soft at first. But it grew stronger, and then a voice began to sing.

"In the sky there is a rainbow . . ."

Willow stood perfectly still, one ear pointed toward their big sisters. Delia held her breath.

"Listen to that," Willow gasped. "They actually sound . . ."

"Good!" Delia said. And this time, she really meant it.

The whole yard had quieted down to hear them. Darlene's voice was a little timid at first. But as Violet played with more confidence, Darlene's singing grew strong and sweet.

They were just hitting their stride when shouting interrupted them. Violet stopped strumming, and Darlene's voice trailed off into the muggy air. All heads turned toward the front of Whispering Pines, where the cars were parked on the gravelly lot.

"Why are those two people running?" someone asked.

"Why are they shouting?" wondered someone else.

"Why is that woman carrying a blue cabbage?" demanded a third.

Delia and Willow craned their necks and stood on their tiptoes to see. Finally, just as the crowd ahead shifted, Delia caught sight of a straw sun hat and a head of wavy-macaroni hair.

"We won!" came Cat's holler. "We took first prize, y'all!"

Mr. Henry bowed politely to Aunt Rosie and Uncle Jonathan, apologizing for interrupting their shower. But they were excited to share their victory with the whole family. Cat was waving the big blue ribbon back and forth.

"We ask you to excuse our enthusiasm," began Mr. Henry, politely addressing the rest of the guests, "but Ms. Catherine and I would be honored to share with you a few jars of our most recent project, Rickles' Prize-Winning Pickles."

Everyone in the yard cheered and applauded for Cat and Mr. Henry. And in no time, the jars were opened and the pickles were passed around to curious guests. Willow and Delia each took one of the long slices as the jars made their way through the crowd, the sour taste causing their lips to pucker.

"Let's make sure Mr. Bacon gets one," Willow said, giving Delia a quick nudge. "He can include Mr. Henry's pickles in his newspaper story about the café!"

As their big sisters began performing again, the cousins made another plate of food to take over to Mr. Bacon, as well as one for Ms. Hightower. Violet's strumming quieted the party guests, and again Darlene's sweet voice drifted up into the humid June air. Her singing was more carefree this time, and Delia could see her sister's confidence growing.

Things were really starting to look up, and Delia

and Willow were smiling as they passed out more cupcakes and lemon bars to guests who were asking for seconds. But all that changed when, suddenly, a single word rang out.

"Fire!"

Chapter 22
it's not a shower without a little water

It wasn't a particularly large fire. Smoke was swirling just above the round table in the center of the yard. And fingers of flame rose from the yellow polka-dotted napkin that had caught fire in the centerpiece candle. It threatened to spread to the whole table, and everyone hurried to step away.

"I've got it," shouted Sweet William over the murmur of the guests. And fixing his goggles over his eyes, he dashed to the hose on the side of the house and turned it on full blast. "Don't worry, Aunt Rosie! I'm ready for the shower!"

And water began to rain down.

It poured onto the table with the burning napkin as well as nearby guests.

It showered onto Delia and Willow and the County Fair judges.

It drenched Aunt Rosie and Uncle Jonathan, Grandma and Grandpa. It sprinkled on the green pickles, the blue ribbon, the yellow flowers, and the silver forks.

And then it soaked the cupcakes and lemon bars and fruit tarts. It even drowned the banana pops.

There wasn't a bit of food spared.

"Turn it off, Sweet William!" called Uncle Liam. "The fire's out! You did your job, now turn off the hose!"

Sweet William, his floaties wrapped around each arm and the snorkel hooked into his mouth, was too busy to hear his father's shouts. He had spent days preparing for Aunt Rosie's shower. He held tight to the long green garden hose in his hand and sprayed straight into the air over the entire party like Chicago's Buckingham Fountain.

But something happened right about then. Delia noticed it first and pointed. Willow followed her finger, and they couldn't help but smile. A hummingbird was hovering near the soaked dessert table, its ruby-red throat catching the light.

"There's a second one," said Willow, pointing toward the porch just behind. "And a third, right above the mushy cupcakes!"

But that wasn't all the cousins noticed just then.

"There's a rainbow!" Delia called to Violet and Darlene, who were dripping and angry like a couple of wet cats, their performance nearly forgotten. "Like in your song!"

And that's when the rest of the crowd noticed too. It was there, in the mist from the hose, arcing high and bright over the whole party. And amid the pointing and gasping and sighing, something else could be heard.

It was laughter.

"At least with that water on, we're not so hot anymore," said one of the aunts. Or maybe it was a family friend, Delia wasn't sure. What she did know was that Sweet William's shower saved the day, in its own strange way. Without it, who knew how fast the fire might have spread? And the last thing they needed was another visit from the fire department.

"That was quite a surprise," chuckled Uncle Jonathan, with his arm around Aunt Rosie.

"Here's another one," she said, rubbing her belly and her back at the same time. "I think we need to go to the hospital!"

And like bees swarming to a flower, Grandma, Aunt Aggie, and Delia's mom were at Aunt Rosie's side. They helped her and Uncle Jonathan race to the car. Gloria Hightower, the hospital president as well as cupcake judge, said she would lead the way. And quick as a bolt of lightning through a summer sky, their cars were down the driveway and pulling onto the road away from Whispering Pines.

Darlene and Violet were left standing front and center, their hair dripping onto their wet shoulders. They looked around for what to do next. The guests did too. Does a baby shower end when the guest of honor rushes off to deliver the baby? Or would it be considered rude to leave until everyone was done celebrating?

Suddenly a real bolt of lightning lit up the sky, and thunder rumbled over the lake. Grandpa and the uncles started waving the whole party toward the Arts & Eats Café.

"Inside, quickly!" they shouted as the skies overhead opened up.

Family and friends held yellow napkins above their heads as they raced for the shelter of the café. In moments, everyone was inside and dripping, grateful for a roof overhead.

Delia pressed in with the rest of the crowd, staring all around at the unusual sight. Every table, every chair—every conceivable space—was occupied. She had never seen the café so full. Cat was behind the counter, passing out cups of coffee. And her dad was explaining one of his paintings to some of Jonathan's relatives.

Delia reached for the ring on her finger and gave it a few turns. What a relief to feel it back on her hand—and to feel the knot in her stomach finally starting to ease.

"The rainbow song! Let's hear you play it again," called Grandpa from the back of the café. And he began to clap for Darlene and Violet. The rest of the guests did too.

"I can't believe how great they sound," Delia told Willow through the cheering. "Like Grandpa said, we *might* have done something good for Darlene and Violet. I think they count as one of our good-luck threes. Or by now, it's fours and even fives!"

They counted them off together. First was Delia's dad and the artwork for the new hospital wing. Second was Chester Bacon's promise to write about the Arts & Eats Café and put it on the front page of the newspaper. And maybe even Delia losing the ring in the first place—if she hadn't, the County Fair judges never would have stopped by.

"Don't forget Aunt Rosie going off to have the

baby," Willow reminded.

"And getting my ring back," Delia added. "That's at least six, right?"

"Oh," hollered Willow, "riding in the fire truck to the County Fair!"

"And seeing the three hummingbirds," Delia said, nearly shouting. "Those are always lucky."

The desserts for the baby shower were in there somewhere too, though the bad luck with the fire and Sweet William's hose made keeping track a little tricky.

"And this," Delia said, looking all around them. "A packed café!"

"In the sky there is a rainbow . . ."

As their sisters played one more round, and the rain beat a rhythm on the windowpanes, Delia looped her arm through Willow's. Even though nobody had thought they could do any cooking this week, even though they hadn't won that blue ribbon at the County Fair, and even though all their desserts had just gotten drenched, things had still worked out.

The shower guests were singing along with their sisters. And Bernice was too, her head tilted back and howling.

Delia pressed on her cheeks, which were starting to ache from smiling so much. "I wonder if this is how fairy godmothers feel at the end of a good day," she said, nudging her shoulder playfully into Willow's.

And together, the two cousins joined in with Bernice and the others, singing extra loud when they got to Delia's favorite verse—the one about how, sometimes, dreams really did come true after all.

oh, baby, what a secret!

With Saturday's baby shower behind them and Sunday true to its name—a sunny day—Delia and Willow spent as much time as they could on the beach. Now it was Monday afternoon, and Willow was supposed to go home in the next day or so, though she and Delia had already begun begging their parents to extend the vacation another week. Or two. Maybe three?

Even Bernice seemed happy for the better weather, running along the water's edge chasing seagulls and digging deep holes in the sand near Grandpa.

"Where's Gossie this morning, Sweet William?"

asked Darlene as they stretched out in the shallow water, letting the waves cover and uncover their legs. "Shouldn't she be down here with us?"

Sweet William pushed his goggles to his forehead and gave Darlene and Violet a serious look.

"Delia helped me move Gossie back to her broccoli bush in the garden," he began. "She said it's better for the goose eggs to be tucked in there than in a cardboard box in the kitchen."

Delia ran her hand through her little cousin's crazy hair.

"It's kind of how Willow and I are," Delia told him. "If we can't be in the Whispering Pines kitchen, well, the next best place is Cat's garden, the great big yard, or down here at the beach!"

They kept playing until lunchtime, when their stomachs let them know it was time to head back up the bluff stairs for something to eat. Grandpa was the first to start the climb, followed closely by Bernice, then Violet and Darlene. Sweet William, Willow, and Delia brought up the rear.

"It's been two days since Aunt Rosie had the baby," Willow was saying. "I wonder when we'll finally meet our new cousin. I can't believe they won't tell us whether it's a boy or a girl."

"I'm still hoping it's a boy," said Sweet William, flopping up the staircase in his bright yellow flippers. "Or maybe a puppy."

Delia couldn't wait either, though she thought it was strange that Aunt Rosie and Uncle Jonathan wanted to keep it such a secret. They weren't letting the cousins know anything until they brought the baby to Whispering Pines to meet the whole family in person.

Chapter 24
the best three months of the year

Once they reached the top of the bluff stairs, Delia and Willow headed straight for the kitchen, while Sweet William started off for Cat's garden to check on Gossie in the broccoli bush. Their big sisters plopped down on the porch steps beside their dads, who were stretched out and looking exhausted.

Grandma was back from the hospital. And she had already put Uncle Liam and Delia's dad to work in the yard, battling weeds that she believed were threatening her newly planted garden. She sat fanning herself with a cluster of blue cornflowers, her broad sun hat ringed with yellow daisies.

"Grandma," Delia began, kneeling beside the wicker chair, "I want to apologize for something."

"I already forgive you," Grandma said, gently brushing her hand against Delia's cheek. "Mistakes happen. And now that it's back on your finger again, I know you'll take extra care of that ring."

Delia threw her arms around her grandmother's shoulders. Somehow Grandma always knew what she and Willow were thinking without them ever having to say it. Not only would Delia be extra careful not to lose her heirloom again, but she would treasure it that much more.

The dads sat nearby on the steps, wiping their sweaty foreheads and gulping down cold lemonade.

"Want us to make some lunch?" Willow asked. "You two look like you could use some food."

"How about sandwiches?" Delia said. "We could let everyone try our latest jam—it's blueberry."

Their dads said that sounded perfect. And in a matter of minutes, Delia and Willow returned to the porch with a platter piled high with peanut-butter-and-homemade-jam triangles.

Only suddenly, there was more family pouring into the yard from the front of the house.

"What have we here?" said Grandpa with surprise. "Looks like a bouquet of babies."

And that's what it seemed to Delia too. She and Willow jumped to their feet, followed closely by Darlene and Violet. They dashed down the porch steps onto the lawn where Aunt Rosie was standing. She was holding a pink bundle in her arms. Beside her stood Aunt Aggie, tears streaming down her face, as she held tight to a second pink bundle. And beside her was Delia's mom, only the bundle in her arms was wrapped in blue.

"I'm so happy everyone is here," Uncle Jonathan began, and he delicately put his arms around Aunt Rosie and her sisters, as if trying to hug all six of the moms and babies at once. "Because we'd like to introduce you to the latest Bumpus family cousins."

"Three!" Delia exclaimed. "Three new cousins?"

"How could you keep such a big secret?" wondered

Willow, who was bouncing so much, she finally kicked off her flip-flops into the bushes. "Three is our good-luck number!"

The three Bumpus sisters pressed in close to the whole family and introduced the tiny new cousins, who were sound asleep.

"What did you name them?" asked Violet softly. "Are they flowers and trees, like us?"

"Or all the same letter," said Darlene, "like us?"

Aunt Rosie and Uncle Jonathan shook their heads.

"We decided to name them after our favorite time of year," he said.

"So you're calling them Summer . . . ?" began Willow slowly.

Aunt Rosie turned the first baby toward Willow and Delia, and she pulled the blanket back just a bit so they could see her sleeping face.

"This is baby June," she whispered.

"And this is July," said Aunt Aggie, tilting the pink bundle in her arms so everyone could see.

"And this little guy is baby August," said Delia's mom, holding the blue blanket forward so everyone could peek into his sleeping face too.

Uncle Liam laughed and said Sweet William should be happy, since he'd been wishing for a boy cousin all along.

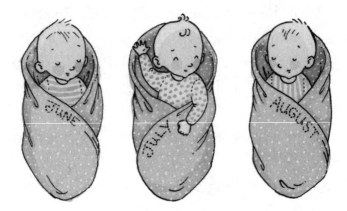

"Where is Sweet William?" asked Aunt Aggie in alarm. "Isn't he around here?"

And as all heads turned, first to the left and then to the right, a honking rang out in the yard. It was followed by busy chirping, along with a gentle woof.

"Delia, look what happened!" shouted Sweet William, marching around the far side of the house from Cat's vegetable garden like he was leading a circus parade. Bernice was beside him, leaping back and forth for joy, her tail wagging wildly.

Behind them waddled a proud Gossie, her beak

held high as she honked and flapped. And following Gossie in the parade were three fluffy yellow goslings, black beaks open and cheeping, tiny webbed feet trying to get the hang of walking. Each one was even cuter than the next.

"You have got to be kidding," moaned Aunt Aggie. "No more pets!"

But everyone else seemed perfectly happy to welcome Gossie's babies into the ever-growing Bumpus family.

"That broccoli bush really did the trick, didn't it?" laughed Cat beside Mr. Henry. He was taking off his sun hat in surprise, then putting it right back on again.

Aunt Rosie and the others bent low and gave Sweet William his own introduction to June, July, and August. And he placed a gentle kiss on each of his new cousins' foreheads—though he seemed to whisper a quick secret into August's ear. Delia figured it was probably a promise about finding frogs together.

Then Grandpa asked Sweet William to introduce his own triplets to the family.

"Well, don't go making fun of their names for being so different," he began shyly. "But I'm calling them Bill, Pat, and Jimmy."

After lots of peeping and cheering, laughing and barking, the whole family climbed the steps onto the Whispering Pines porch. There were plenty of chairs for everybody, and the babies were gently passed from one family member to the next.

"I'm so sorry I left the baby shower in such a rush," Aunt Rosie began. "But I want to thank you for putting out the fire, Sweet William. You were very quick-thinking."

Sweet William said it was nothing. And he pulled his goggles back down over his eyes and looked embarrassed for all the attention.

"And I missed your whole song," Aunt Rosie told Darlene and Violet. "I hear you're going to play at the café this summer. Are you calling yourselves the Raindrops?"

"Or maybe the Umbrellas," Willow suggested, "since that's what everybody wanted at the shower . . ."

"And umbrellas fit with your rainbow song," added Delia. She waited for Violet or Darlene to make that *pfff* sound and say their idea was terrible.

But much to Delia's surprise, Darlene and Violet actually looked as if they liked their suggestion. Darlene said it sounded catchy. And Violet nodded her approval.

"It's official, then," they announced, "we're the Umbrellas!"

Grandpa suggested the Umbrellas play now for Aunt Rosie and for the babies too. "They might like hearing your song as much as the rest of us."

Aunt Rosie agreed. "Please, if you don't mind?"

As they took off across the yard toward the yellow house in search of Violet's ukulele, Cat called after them. She said they could print up flyers and hang them around town. "We'll tell everybody to come hear y'all perform this weekend at the café!"

Aunt Rosie turned to Delia and Willow next.

"And you girls," she said, holding on to each of their hands. "You both worked hard in the kitchen this week, even though none of us thought you could. You certainly proved us wrong. I only wish we had something left of it today—something you could bring out and share."

Delia looked at Willow and raised an eyebrow.

Willow looked right back and smiled.

"I think Grandpa and Sweet William won't mind," Delia said. And the two cousins ducked into the Whispering Pines kitchen. They emerged onto the porch just a few moments later carrying a long tray between them.

Thwack!

"We do have something, Aunt Rosie," Delia announced as she and Willow rounded the corner from the kitchen.

Their big sisters were back from next door, puffing and panting after running up and down the stairs and across the lawn so fast. Violet propped the ukulele against the porch railing and scooted in close to see Delia and Willow's latest creation.

"A gingerbread house?" asked Darlene in surprise as she pressed in next to Violet. "But it's not Christmas."

"Actually, there are two," corrected Delia. "And they're summer beach houses."

One had yellow icing and a sign leaning against the front with the letters A-R-T spelled out in tiny candies. The other house was tall and white with a wide porch.

"Those five gumdrop people are the five of us cousins," Sweet William explained, pointing at the row of sweets held together by toothpicks. They were lined up side by side on the porch. "Grandpa and I ate the rest."

Suddenly Delia had a great idea. She whispered to Willow, who reached into her pocket and pulled out a handful of colorful jelly beans, the last of Grandpa's stash. They picked out two bright pink ones and another pale blue one. Then they carefully pressed the three jelly beans in with the Gumdrop Gang.

"There," Delia said. "Now it's perfect."

"Eight of us cousins, all together on the porch at Whispering Pines," Willow agreed. "Right where we belong."

Gingerbread Cousins

Making and decorating cookies can be a fun activity for the whole family. Using different colored icing, you can decorate your cookies to have Willow's crazy orangey-red curls or Delia's perfect black braid. Or you could decorate them to look like your own family.

Ingredients:

¾ cup molasses
⅓ cup packed brown sugar
⅓ cup water
½ cup (1 stick) butter, softened

3¼ cups all-purpose flour
1 teaspoon baking soda
1½ teaspoons ground ginger
½ teaspoon ground cloves
½ teaspoon ground cinnamon

Directions:

1. Make sure you have an adult's help.

2. Heat the oven to 350 degrees.

3. Using an electric mixer, blend together the molasses, brown sugar, water, and softened butter. Mix until smooth.

4. In a separate bowl, mix the flour, baking soda, ginger, cloves, and cinnamon. Pour the dry ingredients in with the wet, and mix together to form a ball. Wrap the ball in plastic wrap and chill for at least 2 hours in the refrigerator.

5. On a lightly floured surface, roll the dough out to ¼-inch thickness. Using gingerbread boy and girl shapes, cut out cookies.

6. Place shapes onto a cookie sheet lined with parchment paper.

7. Bake for about 12 minutes. Let cool.

8. Decorate with gumdrops, jelly beans, and frosting, and eat up your whole family!

Kate Hannigan loves to test new recipes on her husband, three kids, and even the family dog. When she's not creating disasters in her Chicago kitchen, she's usually at her desk writing fiction and nonfiction for young readers. Kate is also the author of *Cupcake Cousins* and *The Detective's Assistant*. Say hello online at katehannigan.com.

Brooke Boynton Hughes grew up in Loveland, Colorado, where she spent lots of time drawing cats, mermaids, and tree houses. Today, she still lives in Colorado and holds a BFA in Printmaking from Colorado State University and an MFA in Figurative Art from the New York Academy of Art. Brooke is also the illustrator of *Cupcake Cousins* and *Baby Love*. Visit her online at brookeboyntonhughes.com.